"MAQUIS SHIP, THIS IS CAPTAIN BENJAMIN SISKO . . .

"You have not been cleared for approach. If you do not respond immediately, we will assume you to be hostile and respond accordingly." There was a moment of silence as Sisko's threat hung in the air.

Abruptly, a female voice crackled back over the ether. "That will not be necessary, Captain."

Sisko frowned. "Identify yourself."

"We're getting a visual transmission," Dax said.

"On screen," the captain told her. The image of the Maquis ship rippled and was replaced by the face of a determined-looking Bajoran. Kira blinked in surprise.

"I am Ro Laren," the Bajoran said. And with more than a touch of irony, she added, "Perhaps you've heard of me."

STAR TREK
DEEP SPACE NINE®

WRATH OF THE PROPHETS

Peter David, Michael Jan Friedman, and Robert Greenberger

POCKET BOOKS

New York   London   Toronto   Sydney   Tokyo   Singapore

An *Original* Publication of POCKET BOOKS

POCKET BOOKS, a division of Simon & Schuster Inc.
1230 Avenue of the Americas, New York, NY 10020

STAR TREK is a Registered Trademark of Paramount Pictures.

A VIACOM COMPANY

This book is published by Pocket Books, a division of Simon & Schuster Inc., under exclusive license from Paramount Pictures.

ISBN: 0-671-53817-9

First Pocket Books printing May 1997

10 9 8 7 6 5 4 3 2 1

Printed in the U.S.A.

This one's for Katie, who remains steadfast in her love and enthusiasm whenever Daddy starts one of these books   —Bob

For Kalliope   —Mike

@#$%&*!!!   —Peter

AUTHORS' NOTES

This book was tougher than its predecessors (*Doomsday World* and *The Disinherited*—still in print, so go buy them) in that we had to find a reasonable point in the unfolding saga of *Deep Space Nine* to place the story. As you'll see, this takes place after Sisko becomes a captain, but before Worf's arrival on the station.

People ask how three guys can manage to write a book simultaneously (yup, that's how we do it) and the answer is . . . practice. By now, we have a good understanding of what each writer brings to the table and which elements of a novel we can expect from each other.

I have always been the initial idea man, spinning a yarn designed to be broken into three segments (or more, in the case of *Doomsday World*, where Carmen Carter was a collaborator as well).

Mike is the thoughtful polisher, examining how the three components best come together, sanding a spot here or adding some filler there, and then welding it shut so it looks seamless to the casual observer. Peter brings to the partnership a sense of energy and usually comes up with the running themes and gags that allow a novel to breathe. His characterizations and dialogue also keep me and Mike on our toes, pushing us to avoid the routine wherever possible.

Once a thoroughly prepared outline is completed and approved by the understanding Paula Block at Paramount, we divvy up the three segments, each of us fighting for the character arc that interests him the most. (As usual, we're not going to tell you who got what, so you can approach us at conventions and tender your guesses.) There were extremely few new-to-the-fold characters on which to draft background, nor did they commingle as much as in our previous joint efforts, so we were able to skip that phase. We double-checked a few final facts, signed our contracts, and began work.

The biggest complication this time around was Time itself. As in the Jim Croce song, there never seemed to be enough of it. Mike was committed to a schedule for the by-now bestselling hardcover *Kahless* and the DS9 novel *Saratoga*, and Peter spent most of the latter half of 1995 in Montreal, overseeing his TV series *Space Cases* (still airing on Nickelodeon) while completing his work on Jimmy Doohan's bio, *Beam Me Up, Scotty.* And I still had my day job at DC Comics to keep things interesting.

Now, let the thank-yous begin. First, with editor emeritus Kevin Ryan, who gave us a chance to team up again and kept the schedule as flexible as possible. Second, a big thanks to John Ordover, who remained patient and supportive as we petitioned for extension after extension—so that an October deadline became a January deadline and then a June deadline without too much screaming or loss of hair.

Peter, of course, thanks his family: the ever-loyal Myra and daughters Jenny, Shana, and Ariel.

Mike tips his hat to his family as well—his lovely wife Joan and sons Brett and Drew. He would also like to acknowledge the example of Doc Gooden, who showed us the human spirit can endure the roughest of times and still shine.

As for me . . . I'd like to thank my family, too. (Are you starting to see a pattern here?) In this case, the ever-patient Deb and enthusiastic Katie and Robbie. I also appreciate the patience of my DC boss, Terri Cunningham, and my long-suffering assistant, Liz Seward.

Finally, but certainly not least, a big thanks to you, the readers, who have encouraged us all along and always seem to find the right things to say. You've been there to let us know when we were on target and when we might have done something just a bit better. We appreciate those comments (especially the complimentary ones) and look forward to your feedback here—especially since we're serving up the meeting between Lieutenant Ro and Major Kira, the one you've been clamoring for since *DS9* debuted.

We'll see you next in the Delta Quadrant as we complete our tour with a Voyager book—just as soon as a really good idea blossoms into a proposal, which begets a contract, which spawns a manuscript, which is born into a paperback . . .

And so on.

—Bob Greenberger
Connecticut,
June 1996

WRATH OF THE PROPHETS

Prologue

THE SMELL IN the tavern was not insignificant.

A meeting place for all manner of underhanded, disenfranchised, slightly shady, and outright unscrupulous sorts—in short, barterers of everything from bodies to souls—it was situated just off the main boulevard of downtown Sorshaq. Sorshaq was not one of the main cities of Bajor, but that was a matter of choice rather than happenstance, for the residents of Sorshaq tended to keep to themselves. Like shadows, certain insects, and—some joked—various members of the Bajoran provisional government, Sorshaq did better in the darkness than in the light.

The tavern had no other name than "the Place." Brigands and scoundrels, dubious traders and cut-rate brides-of-all-men, would simply say "Meet me at the

Place," and anyone who was in the know would show up there. Anyone who wasn't in the know had no business being there in the first place.

As for the smell . . . no one was entirely sure just what it might be. It seemed to defy description. There was some good old-fashioned sweat, mixed in with free-floating smoke.

Added to that was a dash of blood. Apparently, the management had never quite managed to get the stain out of the floorboards, no matter how hard they tried.

The lighting was dim, as were the waiters and waitresses. But they weren't hired for their brains. The ceiling was low and tended to spring leaks during heavy rains. This was actually something of a blessing because the rainy season was pretty much the only time the floor got washed.

One would have thought that the Place would do the bulk of its business at night, but that was not the case. Rather, the Place was busy all day and all evening with a fairly consistent crowd throughout.

It was about midday, and the Place was deep in its customary hustle and bustle, when the door swung open and a short but heavyset Terran strode in. "Afternoon, everybody," called the Earthman.

A shout of "Gnome!" went up from all and sundry. "Gnome" was not his real name, of course. Then again, most people in the Place tended to be hailed by some pseudonym or nom de guerre. It tended to simplify matters, particularly if the authorities were sniffing around in search of someone specific. One's real name tended to stick with one, but a false one could be discarded and replaced on a moment's notice.

Gnome sauntered across to the bar and sidled up to the Bajoran bartender. "So you're back in town, Gnome?" asked the bartender, whose name was Sandon.

Gnome gave him a pitying, even patronizing look, since the answer to the question was rather self-evident. "What tipped you off?" he asked.

Sandon smiled gamely. "Gnome, you're such a kidder," he said, which was what he always said when Gnome had made a statement that had gone over his head. "Got something cooking?"

"You could say that," said Gnome. "Looking for someone. A lady by the name of Varis. A Bajoran. Anyone come by and identify herself by that name?"

Sandon shook his head.

"Well." Gnome sighed. "Maybe she'll be along soon." He rapped on the bar in front of him, which was all he needed to do to indicate he wanted a drink to occupy that space.

Sandon complied. "Hey," he said. "Got one for you. What's the difference between a black hole and the Bajoran High Council?"

Gnome shrugged. "I give up. What?"

Sandon was about to reply when he heard one particular customer, a Tellarite, raise his voice to an extremely loud and annoying level. Not only was he bothering other customers, but he was making it impossible for Sandon to finish the joke.

So the bartender pulled out a disruptor from under the bar and shot him.

The Tellarite uttered a screech and then fell forward over the table. There was a brief smattering of applause, and while a waitress cleaned off the table, Sandon turned back to Gnome. "Where was I?"

"The difference between a black hole and the Bajoran High Council."

"Oh, right. Okay, the answer is: one of them sucks in everything and gives back nothing . . . and the other is a dead star."

Gnome smiled thinly. "Make that up yourself?"

"Yup," said Sandon proudly.

"I could tell."

Sandon studied him quizzically for a moment and then his face brightened. "Gnome, you're such a kidder," he said.

At that moment the door to the Place opened, and everyone turned to glance in the direction of the new arrival.

She was wearing simple traveling garments and a hood that obscured most of her face. It was clear, however, that she was Bajoran. She hesitated, then looked around, her eyes narrowing to accommodate the difference in light between the bright sunshine outdoors and the dimness of the Place's interior.

The fact that she didn't back down from the olfactory ambiance of the Place garnered her a few quick respect points from the regulars.

Gnome cast a silent glance at Sandon and moved off toward his customary table. The glance was filled with meaning; Sandon was to tactfully probe the female's reason for showing up at the Place. If she passed muster and was indeed who Gnome was supposed to be meeting, then Sandon would forward her to Gnome himself.

Gnome sat down, the chair creaking slightly under his weight, and nursed his drink as he watched Sandon engage the young woman in conversation. He was quite accomplished at appearing friendly and conversational, yet also rather good at extracting needed information. The exchange lasted several minutes.

And then, as Gnome watched with ever-suspicious eyes, Sandon made a head-nodding gesture in Gnome's direction. The young woman turned toward Gnome. Their gazes met.

Gnome was skilled at assessing people's state of mind just from a quick glance into their eyes, and this case was no exception. The young woman had an unmistakable nervousness in her eyes, but by the same token there was an undercurrent of strength. She was clearly determined to try and mask her apprehension.

With a lesser judge of character than Gnome, she might well have succeeded. As it was, her mild agitation was obvious to him.

The woman crossed the room, slid into the seat opposite him, and said softly, "You are the Gnome?"

Gnome nodded. "And you are Varis?"

"Yes. Where is it?"

He smiled broadly. "You like to get right down to it, don't you?"

"I see no reason to delay," she said briskly. "Do you have what I came for?"

"Yes. What I don't have is the payment."

"Half the credit transfer has already been made, and the rest will be attended to on delivery."

He studied her as a scientist might study a microbe. "How do I know you can be trusted?"

She reached into the folds of her robe and pulled out a small blinking transmission device.

"Let me guess," he said. "That's a triggering device for a bomb. If you don't get what you want immediately, you'll blow us all to kingdom come."

Varis looked at him with a mixture of pity and amazement. "Prophets, how you think. No . . . this is a computer link. I'm already hooked into the financial system. The transfer is ready. All I have to do is punch in the authorization code, and the funds will be released to the sources you indicated. You can then contact your sources and verify the transfer. Will that satisfy you?"

Gnome drummed his thick fingers on the table for a moment, and then he rose without a word. "Come along," he told Varis and headed for the door. The young woman followed him.

Once they were out in the open air, Varis took the opportunity to suck in a huge lungful of air—though she tried not to make it obvious. Nevertheless, Gnome noticed. It was clear that the atmosphere in the Place had been repulsive to her, but she had held up anyway. Apparently, she had sensed that weakness was simply not an option when dealing with people like Gnome.

Gnome considered her for a moment. He knew little about her other than the basic information he'd been given in order to carry through the deal.

In his organization, no one ever had all the information. That was as it should be, since it meant that any interrogation upon capture could only yield dribs and drabs of information—but not enough to do any real damage to the organization itself.

What he *did* know was this: her family name was Varis, she was connected somehow with a small village to the east, and the village was having problems.

Then again, mused Gnome, what village on Bajor wasn't having problems? Sandon and his peers could make all the jokes about government they wanted, but the situation was far from funny. Everyone in the quadrant knew that the Bajoran government was in complete disarray.

Dozens of petty bureaucrats and self-aggrandizing politicos had tried to establish power bases for themselves. Serving the people, after all, was a far less interesting pastime than serving oneself.

The war-torn planet was bleeding from the wounds it had sustained under Cardassian rule, and now it was hemorrhaging out its economy.

And if you lived in a small starving village, you

were just out of luck. Your needs had to wait until the government got around to attending to them. With things the way they were, that could be a hideously long time.

What all of it boiled down to was that concerned citizens such as Varis, eager to do whatever they could to help their fellow Bajorans, were often moved to take desperate measures—like dealing with Gnome.

He moved quickly and expertly through the streets, Varis hurrying to keep up with him. Finally he stopped outside a building that even the relatively inexperienced Varis could identify as a hangar bay.

Gnome entered a combination into the lock and the door promptly slid open. He looked right and left, making a great show of exaggerated subterfuge, and then sidled into the room. Varis likewise looked around, unsure of why she was doing so, but positive that there must be a reason for it. Once inside, the door slid shut behind them.

Inside the building was a large runabout. It looked somewhat tired, which prompted a bit of a scowl from Varis. Gnome, however, looked upon his "seasoned" craft pas a badge of honor, and he patted its side affectionately.

"I've run more than a couple of Federation block-ades with this baby," he said.

"It shows," Varis responded doubtfully.

"Care to inspect the cargo?"

Varis nodded and followed him in. The light inside the runabout was dim, although not quite as dark as it had been in the Place. However, her eyes seemed to adjust more quickly than before.

There were transport containers in the back. She went to one and cracked it open, her fingers practically clawing it. First she looked inside, then back to him.

"This is it," she said with excitement.

Gnome nodded. "Replicators and the raw materials required to make . . . well, to make whatever the latest Bajoran cuisine is. No offense, but your food always gives me the trots. Now . . . the credit transfer, if you please?"

"Of . . . of course." Varis removed the padd from her robes and typed in a series of codes. She waited a moment for a response, and then it began to blink with serene confidence. "All right. It's done."

"Give me a moment," he said, and moved to the communications board inside his ship.

As Varis opened the other crates and found more of the same, her head began to spin. She felt short of breath.

It was going to work. It was actually going to work. She was going to save her people, and . . .

Gnome approached her and began replacing the lids on the cartons. She looked up at him in confusion.

"What?" she asked. "What? The transfer went through, didn't it?"

"Oh, yes," he told her. "It went through. But there's a bit of a problem."

She clutched one of the large lids to herself. "What sort of problem?"

He smiled an oily smile. "Well, you see, the price has gone up."

"Gone up." Her voice sounded odd to her. "It . . . can't have gone up. The price was agreed upon."

"Yes," he agreed, "but I had to take some additional risks in order to get it here." Gnome stroked his chin. "It added costs. Interest, you might say, upon your original investment." He paused, then put a hand roughly on her shoulder.

Varis's eyes narrowed, still clutching the lid to her chest.

Suddenly a hole appeared in the lid she was clutching. The hole had been made by a phaser blast from the weapon she held in her small but steady hand.

Gnome rocked back on his heels, stumbled, and then crashed heavily against a container, knocking it over. If the phaser had been on one of its higher settings, he would not have survived the experience. As it was, he was simply stunned. When he woke up, it was going to be with one hell of a headache.

And without his ship.

It took all of Varis's strength to lift the black marketeer halfway to a sitting position and drag him across the ground. She had not planned on this turn of events, but neither had she been completely unprepared for it. Hauling him over to the open hatchway, she pitched him out. Gnome thudded to the floor of the hangar bay and rolled a couple of feet before stopping.

"I'll be borrowing your ship," she called to his unconscious form. "Consider it a penalty for your behavior." Then she closed the hatch and sat down at the controls.

Varis was feeling a great deal older than her nineteen years.

She studied the runabout controls. Thanks to her friendship with Jake Sisko, they weren't completely alien to her. During her time at *Deep Space Nine,* Jake had decided to show off for her a bit by taking her aboard a runabout and explaining how it all worked.

They hadn't left the station, of course. But Jake— the picture of confidence—had shown her how to maneuver through a combination of ion storms and meteor showers without sustaining damage.

When she had first arrived on *Deep Space Nine,* Varis had been nothing more than a scared fifteen-year-old, thrust into the leadership of her Paqu village after her parents had been killed by Cardassians. As *tetrarch,* it had fallen upon her to negotiate land boundaries with representatives of the rival Navot village. It was her friendship with Jake and the little Ferengi known as Nog that had enabled her to solve her problems with the Navot.

Varis sighed. She had hoped to prevail upon the black marketeer to transport her back to her village. To perform, in essence, a favor on top of the financial arrangement into which they had entered.

Upon reflection, she now saw how naive she had been. A creature like Gnome had no "better nature" to which she could have appealed.

Her hands fluttered over the ship's controls for a moment. Jake called such things "idiot-proof." They had been designed, through years of careful craftsmanship, to be simple to use.

With a confidence born of self-assurance and ignorance, Varis quickly activated the thrusters. The runabout lifted off the ground with only the slightest of herky-jerky movements, and then the engines roared as the ship hurtled forward.

At which point, Varis suddenly realized that she had neglected to open the door to the hangar bay.

As the runabout smashed through the door, she had a quick glimpse of passersby ducking to shield themselves from flying pieces of debris, and then Varis realized that she was on a direct collision course with a building directly across the way. Residents of the building saw her coming and leaped out of their windows to avoid the imminent collision.

Varis pulled on the controls as fast and as hard as she could. The nose of the runabout abruptly angled upward—at nearly a ninety-degree angle, the Bajoran sun glinting off the vessel's windshield. And the vessel soared toward the heavens like a great wingless angel.

Yes, an angel, most definitely that. An angel of mercy, on her way to help her people.

By casting herself in that role, she realized that she was able to forgive herself for circumventing the laws of Bajor that she had sworn to uphold as a tetrarch. She could forgive herself for dealing with black marketeers, and she could forgive herself for stealing a runabout as well.

She could forgive herself all that because Varis Sul, tetrarch of the Paqu, believed in the rightness of her course. She had seen her people needy, starving. They had looked to her in silent supplication; silent because they were a resolute, uncomplaining people, who saw no need to heap guilt and frustration upon their leader.

Responding to their quiet desperation, she had gone to the government. It had been no use. She had approached Jake Sisko and his father, the commander of *Deep Space Nine*. No use again.

In fact, no one had been of any use, least of all her. She finally had decided that she was not going to tolerate it any longer. And as a result, she found herself flying a stolen runabout filled with contraband replicators and the raw material they needed. Only the Prophets knew where Gnome had gotten them. From a shipment intended for a space station? Scavenged, perhaps, from a space vessel that had been seized, its crew slaughtered, but its equipment left intact?

Once upon a time, Varis would have dwelt heavily on such things. But now it would be a luxury to do so—a philosophical and moral nicety she could no longer afford.

She felt the weaker for her calm attitude. She felt unclean, in fact. But that didn't matter. Nothing mattered except helping her people.

Perhaps her actions were sinful. But she didn't care. As the ground sped past beneath her, she mused that if morals and a clear conscience were in short supply, well, at least help was to be had in abundance. And ultimately, that was all that mattered.

* * *

When Varis Sul arrived at her village, the rejoicing that followed was incredible. The feast her people put on was dazzling beyond anything within Paqu memory. The replicators, hooked up quickly, churned out food with breathtaking speed, and even that was insufficiently rapid for the starving populace.

Originally, tables had been set up for people to sit at in a civilized way. But that idea quickly went by the wayside as people plopped down to gorge themselves anywhere they could. Streets, sidewalks, under trees and bushes.

Even the animals were fed. The crops that were the animals' sustenance had been particularly bad in the past year—just another aspect of a situation that had seemed completely hopeless.

There was laughter and rejoicing, music and dancing and food, always more food. And the songs . . .

Songs of celebration, of thanks. And all of them were dedicated to, and sung about, Varis Sul. New songs were fabricated on the spot, and old songs were intoned about great old heroes, with Varis Sul's name substituted in the appropriate places.

Thanks to the Bajoran troubadours, Varis Sul was credited with everything from defeating the Cardassians to the creation of the planet itself.

But Varis heard none of these. Despite the urging of her neighbors, she did not participate. She ate, of course, although nowhere near as much as everyone else. Instead, she ate a small portion, with the intent of visiting the temple afterward.

And there she would pray for forgiveness.

Which, unfortunately for her, and all the people in her town . . . wouldn't come. Something else was coming instead.

A considerable smell would soon fill the Paqu village, just as it had the Place. It would be the stink of fear.

CHAPTER
1

Kneeling on the floor in a corner of the station's operations center, Miles O'Brien checked his tricorder, hoping to see a steady line on its sensor readout.

Unfortunately, the line he saw had a power spike at three-second intervals. He used the back of his hand to wipe a thin film of sweat from his forehead and spoke to the engineering assistant halfway inside the bulkhead.

"We've got the spike again, Tony," the chief said with resignation. "Try switching the power relays for the OHD."

Tony Kwiatkowski, a thin wiry man with a large nose and dark hair, pulled himself out of the bulkhead. "Don't you mean the ODN, sir?"

O'Brien's face flushed with embarrassment. There was a big difference between an optical data network and an omnidirectional holographic diode.

"Yeah," he admitted, "I guess I do."

His assistant chuckled, then crawled back into the bulkhead to see it done. The chief shook his head at the mistake. He didn't make them very often, after all. But then, he wasn't often as distracted as he was now.

Keiko and Molly, his wife and little daughter, had returned only the day before from Bajor, where Keiko had been involved in a long and demanding botanical expedition. Back on the *Enterprise,* it had been possible for O'Brien and his bride to pursue their respective careers and still see each other every night. That wasn't the case on *Deep Space Nine.*

As chief of operations, O'Brien was always mired knee-deep in repairs, slowly and laboriously correcting the mindless damage the Cardassians had inflicted before they left the station. To make matters worse, it was his job to meld existing Cardassian systems with newly introduced Federation technology.

All in all, a demanding job. And one that didn't allow him to take much time off.

Keiko, on the other hand, couldn't be much of a botanist on *Deep Space Nine.* Her job entailed a great deal of field work. Hence, the long periods of time spent in the Bajoran wilderness.

With Molly. *Without* O'Brien.

But now they were home, and life was good again. Full. Complete.

"Chief?" came Kwiatkowski's voice, muffled by his confinement.

O'Brien leaned over to peer inside. "What is it?" he asked.

His assistant smiled as he pointed to the ODN juncture, a bulky box in which raw power was converted for use by a half-dozen tertiary systems.

"I've replaced the relays. How does it look?"

The chief used his tricorder to monitor the power flow. "Damn," he said.

"The spikes are still there?" Kwiatkowski asked.

"Still there," O'Brien confirmed.

He had hoped to have settled the problem an hour ago. Now, instead of spending some time with his family before dinner, he'd be lucky to get to his quarters before the food got cold.

Abruptly, he made an executive decision. "That's it," he said. "We'll pick up on this tomorrow."

His assistant looked at him as if he'd grown a second head. "But sir . . ." he began.

"I know," O'Brien said, "I know." It wasn't like him to give up on a problem until he'd gotten it licked. "But tonight is special—my first dinner with my wife and daughter in months. I'm not going to miss it for anything short of a station-wide emergency."

Which this definitely wasn't. Thanks to the chief's dedication over the last few years, there were plenty of backup systems that could carry the load until the next morning.

Kwiatkowski shrugged. "You're the boss," he said.

O'Brien smiled. He was, wasn't he? And for once the boss was going home right on time.

As soon as his assistant wriggled out of the bulkhead again, the two men wrestled the corresponding junction plate back into place. And when Kwiatkowski volunteered to put their tools away, the chief was only too happy to accept the offer.

Crossing Ops, he headed for the nearest turbolift.

All the while Keiko and Molly had been off-station, O'Brien had dreaded going back to his quarters at night. Usually, he shared a meal at Quark's place with Julian Bashir, then found a reason to remain in the bar the rest of the evening.

Sure, he had regained his old form at darts against Bashir and polished up on his kayaking skills in the holosuites. But in the end, he'd always had to go home to an empty echoing set of walls.

Not now, he told himself. Not for a while, at least. As far as he was concerned, the longer the better.

As he entered the turbolift, O'Brien allowed his mind to drift, thinking of things he could do with Molly in the days to come. There would be a zoo trip, thanks to the reservations he'd made in Quark's holosuite. Also a sailing excursion, and then a circus as well.

He kept arranging and rearranging the order of events in his mind, oblivious to his whereabouts.

So when he realized he was standing in front of the door to his quarters, it was with a bit of surprise.

Home, he thought. He had never fully appreciated the meaning of the word until now.

As the doors slid open, the chief heard a clattering of dishes. "Looks like someone's home from work," Keiko called.

O'Brien heard a squeal. Then, as the aroma of dinner came to him, there was a sound of small quick feet and a tiny figure with long dark hair burst out of the other room.

With another squeal, this one louder than the first, Molly threw herself at her father. He snatched her out of midair.

"Daddy! Daddy!" she exclaimed. "Come quickly! I want to show you the picture I made after lunch and then you can see the clay figure I made and the dinner I helped make and then I want a story . . ."

"Hold on, little one," O'Brien said with a laugh. It was one thing to follow a string of technical babble during the heat of battle, but it was quite another to interpret the breathless rush of an excited child.

Hugging Molly to him, he returned his attention to the smell. It was something familiar. And wonderful.

He called out to his wife. "Yankee pot roast! Right, Keiko?"

"Yes, Daddy," said his daughter, before his wife could reply. "With broccoli and ice cream."

Keiko stuck her head around the corner of a bulkhead. "Actually," she told him, "only the broccoli will be served with the pot roast. The ice cream is scheduled for dessert."

O'Brien grinned. "I sort of figured that."

He reveled in the sight of his wife, who somehow always looked more appealing to him every time he saw her. She was wearing something soft and green that hugged her in all the right places. And her eyes were filled with a spark, with the kind of life he had not seen in them since before he took his family off the *Enterprise.*

The chief was delighted with the menu, too, knowing full well Keiko only made a red-meat dish when she wanted to do something special for him. Clearly, she was trying to make up for lost time.

Putting Molly down, he patted her on the rump. "Go get your picture and your clay figure," he told her. "I want to take a look."

As his daughter complied, O'Brien wandered over to the dining area, where his wife was leaning over the replicator. His intention was to hug her for all he was worth.

But with a fluid graceful motion, Keiko whirled around and snuck under his outstretched arms, carrying a hot serving dish. A cloud of steam trailed behind her.

O'Brien shook his head. There would be time for romance later, he supposed. Shrugging, he ordered up a cup of coffee, his fifth of the day.

"Come and sit down, Miles," Keiko told him.

A moment later, Molly arrived with her creations in tow. "Here they are," she said.

The chief oohed and aahed over them, though he hadn't the slightest idea what they were supposed to be. Then he settled Molly into her seat, adjusting a cloth napkin in front of her blue overalls.

Smiling, Keiko arranged the various dishes on the table, then slid into her chair and reached for the serving utensils. O'Brien grinned and took his own seat, savoring the aroma from the meat.

"Smells delicious," he said.

"It should," his wife replied, a serious tone in her voice. "I spent twenty minutes sifting through roast offerings on the menu and then had to edit one to match that meal we had back on the *Enterprise.*" Keiko began to serve Molly her child's portion.

The chief grunted. "Meal? On the *Enterprise?*"

Keiko sighed, her smooth skin furrowing between her eyes. "You're hopeless, you know that? Think about it."

She busied herself fastening Molly's napkin and pouring her a drink. In the meantime, O'Brien searched his memory for the occasion in question. Keiko's exasperation signaled it was a special moment: dear to her, though obviously forgotten by O'Brien.

Then it hit him.

"It's your birthday," he blurted out.

Keiko stared at him wide-eyed. Sighing, she cut up Molly's food for her.

No, thought the chief, that wasn't it. He racked his brain again, scrunching his face in thought. In the meantime, his food sat untouched.

Finally he put it together. "We celebrated my

posting to *Deep Space Nine* with Yankee pot roast," he announced triumphantly, then smiled. "What's going on? I'm not being transferred, am I?"

It was a joke, but Keiko didn't laugh. What's more, her playfulness melted away. O'Brien swallowed. He recognized that look. His wife used it when a subject important to her was about to be broached.

"Well?" he prodded gently.

Keiko sat down as Molly began to eat and directed her full attention toward her husband. "No," he said, "you're staying put. You're happy here."

"And I'm happy to be back here, with you. But . . . an opportunity has come up. The Bajorans I work with contacted me today—"

"No," repeated O'Brien. The word was sharp, direct, intended to preclude any further discussion.

He should have known it wouldn't work. Not on Keiko.

She forged ahead as if he hadn't even spoken. "They've discovered some new kind of flora on a remote island. It's got them stumped as to whether it's a naturally occurring anomaly or something the Cardassians brought with them. Anyway, I—"

"You're not going back," O'Brien insisted. To keep from saying anything further, anything he might regret, he raised his mug to his lips and swallowed some coffee. The heat from the mug made his face flush, but not half as much as the heat of his anger.

His wife leaned forward over the table, as determined as he was. "They need me, Miles. I can't just close off a part of my life, not after living it again for six months. You, you're needed every day and that makes you feel good. I'm proud of you and your accomplishments. But I want to feel good, too—to take pride in some accomplishments of my own."

He had seen that look before, just prior to her last departure. She wasn't going to give in, not for anything.

"I need you," he said softly. "And who'll watch Molly?"

"She'll come back to the planet with me," Keiko said quickly, trying to get the words out. "She made some friends down there, and they'll be at the site, too. Miles, it's only for three weeks at most . . ."

O'Brien shook his head. "I've missed enough of her growing up. We were just about to regain some balance, her and me. Why now?"

"Because they want to know what it is as soon as possible," his wife replied. "They want to know if it's dangerous, if it'll have an impact on the ecosystem . . ."

Her voice trailed off. There was silence for a moment.

O'Brien pushed some of the food around on his plate. Molly had stopped eating and was watching with wide-eyed interest, looking a little scared. He needed to regain his self-control before things turned ugly.

"When do you go?" he asked.

"The next transport leaves tomorrow," Keiko answered. "I've already booked passage." A pause. "I'm sorry, Miles. I don't want to leave so soon, but there's no other way."

"It's just three weeks, Daddy," Molly offered.

Bless her heart, thought O'Brien, she was trying to play peacemaker. Unfortunately, she was much too young to be subjected to that.

He smiled at his daughter. "You see, angel, just a week feels like a very long time when you're not here to keep me company. Three weeks is like . . . like . . ."

It was like forever. But he didn't say it out loud. He only shrugged.

"We'll be back as soon as we can," Molly assured him, sounding mature beyond her years. She turned to Keiko. "Right, Mommy?"

Keiko smiled tenderly. Then she turned to her husband.

"I'll talk to them," she assured him. "One week, no more. We can both live with that, can't we?"

Her eyes didn't leave his. They seemed to be pleading her argument on a quieter level.

O'Brien wanted to see her happy—but not necessarily at the price of his own happiness. Then again, if it was only a week . . .

No, he insisted inwardly. It'll be a week here, a week there, and before you know it she'll be gone *all* the time.

Still, what could he do? How could he stop her?

"Go," he spat. "Study your bloody weed. Abandon me every time they snap their fingers."

Keiko's eyes grew hard. "You mean the way you go running every time they blow a circuit around here? There are other engineers on the station, Miles. They can change a chip once in a while without you."

O'Brien stood up abruptly, knocking his chair over. "I have a responsibility to this station," he told her. "That's the job I agreed to, the job I signed up for."

He was furious. He wanted to say more. But he saw Molly out of the corner of his eye and bit his lip.

"Suddenly," he rasped, maintaining control as best he could, "I don't have much of an appetite."

Turning, he left their quarters. For a while, he was too angry to pay attention to where he was going. Thoughts careened through his mind, crashing and merging so quickly he had no idea what he was really thinking about.

Bajorans. Weeds. Molly's smile. All images imprinted on his mind as he tried to sort things out, calm himself down.

It was no surprise that when he did slow down, O'Brien was near Quark's. Grunting, he walked in and ordered himself a beer.

At least there, he thought, amid the noise and the gaudy lights, he could let off some steam. Then, when he was in control of himself again, he could return to his quarters.

And help his wife pack.

After all, he was determined not to let her leave the station angry at him. He needed her to come back.

CHAPTER
2

IT STARTED SLOWLY, and it began with the animals.

The celebration in the Paqu village had died off, because, of course, there was only so long anyone could sustain such festivities. Nevertheless, there was an overwhelming feeling of joy and contentment.

One of the more popular of the grazing animals among the Paqu was a largish creature called a Rinta. Rintas were not highly regarded for their intelligence. They were slow-moving and rather benign. Their fur color ranged from light to dark red, and their eyes were large and unblinking.

Rintas tended to stay by the river; their need for water was copious. When fed the proper grains, which, thankfully, the replicators were capable of reproducing, they generated a milk that was high in a

28

variety of vitamins essential for proper Bajoran growth and nutrition.

The replicators could have produced that milk as well, of course, but there was only so far they could go in producing the proper taste and texture. And the Bajorans tended to be picky when it came to Rinta milk.

So it was rather surprising, even disturbing, when Varis Sul was summoned from a meeting with village elders one day, not too long after the time of the great feasting. A young farmer named Tres had come to alert Varis to some troubling news: two of the Rintas did not seem to be in especially good shape.

"Rintas never get sick," Varis told him.

This was a sweeping generalization, but fairly accurate. Rintas were long-lived.

So the ill health of one was unusual enough, in and of itself. To learn that two seemed afflicted with some sort of problem bordered on the alarming.

"It's true, Sul," said Tres, and the tetrarch had no reason to doubt his words. She followed the young farmer to the site where Tres's Rintas grazed. As they came over the small hill, Tres was in the lead, and Varis heard him gasp in shock. The tetrarch drew alongside Tres, and her eyes widened in astonishment.

One of the Rintas had collapsed.

It had tumbled into the river and was just lying there, its great chest heaving. The other Rinta looked on with what appeared to be infinite sadness in its large eyes. Varis and Tres ran quickly over to the fallen Rinta, Varis wading into the water to lift the creature's head.

"Help me get her back up onto the shore!" said the tetrarch, and Tres tried his best to comply. But the Rinta seemed to weigh half a ton, and despite Varis and Tres's best effort, they were helpless to hoist the creature out of the water.

"Get help!" barked Varis, and Tres ran.

As the water rolled past them, Varis crouched down and looked deep into the creature's eyes, trying to get some glimmer of understanding as to what the animal was going through.

The great eyes stared at her in a manner that was— what? Confused? Betrayed? Varis couldn't be sure of what was going through the creature's very simple mind.

A thick dark liquid trickled from the Rinta's mouth. Could it be blood, she wondered? Or some sort of bronchial fluid that had collected in the animal's lungs? It dribbled into the river and flowed away. "What's the matter with you?" Varis demanded, as if she could expect the animal to respond with a detailed list of its symptoms and possible illnesses.

And then Varis heard a low animal moan . . . but it wasn't coming from the Rinta whose head she was cradling in the rushing river. Instead it came from the second Rinta, and Varis turned just in time to see—to her alarm—the animal stumble into the river and fall flat into the rushing water.

It generated a huge splash that drenched Varis from

head to hips. She stared in disbelief as the Rinta flopped over and over in the water, writhing as if possessed by some inner demon.

By the time Tres arrived with help, it was too late. One of the Rintas had already died, and the other was clearly in its death throes.

Keiko had just emerged from the bedroom with the last of her research tools when O'Brien's combadge chirped. The chief frowned as he tapped it.

"O'Brien here."

"This is the captain," said Sisko. "Sorry to interrupt, Chief, but we've still got that power flux in the data circuits—and it's registering near the med labs now. This isn't going to help anyone get those reports finished."

O'Brien sighed. "Acknowledged, sir. Be up in just a few minutes."

Molly looked at him patiently. She had long ago learned to stay quiet when Daddy began talking to the air.

"Thanks, Chief. Sisko out."

Suddenly Molly hugged her father fiercely. Lifting her into his arms, O'Brien swallowed hard. He was afraid his little girl would return a teenager and he wouldn't know her. A foolish thought, maybe, but one that afflicted him with increasing frequency.

Packing the last of her belongings, his wife looked at him with mixed emotions on her face. "I'll miss you," she said.

"I'll miss you, too," he assured her.

Keiko walked over to him and hugged him just as hard as Molly had. Miles held the two of them.

"You be good on Bajor," he told his wife. "And be successful as well."

"We'll be back before you know it," she promised.

She had said almost the exact same words when she left the last time. And that became six whole months. If she found something equally intriguing, who knew how long she might be down there?

O'Brien hugged his family a little tighter. He savored their warmth, their breath, their nearness. Then, reluctantly, he let go.

"The captain's waiting for me," he said softly.

Keiko nodded. "We'll be fine. And if I know the captain, he'll keep you so busy you won't realize we're gone until we get back."

The chief grunted. "No doubt," he said, though without much conviction. He leaned over, kissed his wife on the lips, and tousled Molly's dark hair. Then he kissed her, too.

Molly giggled. It made him smile. He decided that was the image he wanted to remember until they got back.

"Go," Keiko advised gently.

"I'm going," he replied.

With a last look at his wife and daughter, O'Brien left them and headed for the infirmary.

Downriver from the Paqu, in the Navot village, residents were using the river as they always did: for bathing and for drinking, though not at the same time, of course. They were unaware of the fluids secreted by the Rintas upstream in the Paqu village, unaware that there was any possible hint of danger.

The Navot crops had been better in the past year than those of the Paqu, a good fortune that the Navot did not question. They wished ill to no one, but their old rivalry with the Paqu couldn't help but give them a feeling of superiority—a sense that they were blessed by the Prophets above all others. For truly, wasn't their life—despite the unrest on Bajor— basically a good life?

Imagine their surprise when their Rintas began to look somewhat under the weather. By the time that happened, however, Tres the Paqu farmer had fallen ill. . . .

"You must speak to them!"

Kai Winn stood with her back to Ompar Tenzil. Ompar was a rather large, singularly aggressive member of the Bajoran government. He was the primary liaison between the secular and the religious order, and Kai Winn found herself wishing for someone who was more . . . sedate, somehow.

Ompar frequently behaved as if he were playing to the back row of a theater. He had just come from speaking with the council of Vedeks, and now he was venting his spleen to the Kai.

But Kai Winn was barely listening to his continued exhortations that she take action. The Bajoran holy woman was instead staring out the window. The view of the countryside that she had always taken for granted looked tainted somehow, though she had no idea how much of it was her own imagination.

"What would you have me say, Ompar?" Kai Winn said tiredly after a time.

"You are the Kai!" he reminded her. "We of the provisional government are trying to prevent a panic from spreading among the people, and are looking to you to help us! You must tell the people," he said, making vague gestures of frustration. "You must tell them this is a test! Yes, that's it!" he continued, thinking quickly as he spoke. "You must tell them this is a test given them by the Prophets!"

As Ompar had no doubt wished all along, the Kai turned and looked at him. "A test?" she repeated in an astonished tone.

"That's right," said Ompar. Having taken a position, he seemed to feel the need to defend it. "It's a test."

"Of what?" asked Winn.

"Their belief," he told her.

"Their belief?" The Kai made a soft clicking sound with her tongue against her teeth. "People and animals are dying, Ompar. What sort of test is that? What sort of belief is being challenged?"

He frowned. "With all due respect, Kai, I think you are overstating the situation . . ."

"With all due respect to *you,* Ompar, I believe I am giving a perfectly accurate assessment," Winn shot back. "There is some sort of disease out there. We've traced its origins to somewhere in the farm lands, but it's spread rapidly beyond that. More and more cases are being reported with each passing day . . . each passing hour, it seems."

She snapped her fingers with a sound like a rifle shot.

"And you're telling me this is supposed to be some sort of test from the Prophets? What are they testing, Ompar? The religious fortitude of our Rintas? Or the resolve of babies, perhaps? It's the babies that drink the most Rinta milk. They and nursing mothers. How is this test administered, and how in the name of heaven are we supposed to pass it?"

Ompar was silent a moment, and then he said darkly, "Perhaps . . . it is not a test, then." And then he paused before adding, "Perhaps . . . it is a punishment."

She looked at him. "For what?"

"I don't know," admitted Ompar. "Do you?"

"Me?" The Kai gave a derisive laugh. "You're asking me to come up with reasons to support your theories."

He gestured helplessly. "Kai . . . we must do something . . ."

She sighed. "I want you to do two things, Ompar. You are in a position of authority; it should be easy. First, I want you to track down the origin of this disease. Saying that it originated in the farm lands is not enough. I have been studying maps, tracking down all the information I can. As near as I can tell, the first reported instances of the disease occurred in the Paqu village. That would be Varis Sul's territory."

She paused, thinking of the aggressive and occasionally headstrong young tetrarch. "Check with Sul, find out if anything unusual was introduced into the village. Report back to me as quickly as possible, for as soon as I have some sort of useful information, I will be consulting with Captain Sisko."

"The Emissary?" said Ompar, making no attempt to hide his disdain. "This is a Bajoran matter . . ."

"These are Bajoran deaths," Kai Winn corrected sharply. "If there is any chance that *Deep Space Nine* can provide us with aid, then it would be unconscionable of me not to explore that option."

Clearly Ompar did not agree, but he saw that it was pointless to argue. After a moment, he asked, "And the second thing you would have me do, Kai?"

"Inform the government," she said slowly, "that we will be holding global prayer meetings. We will pray for strength. We will pray for guidance. We will pray for our doctors to discover a cure for this hideous affliction. And we will pray for the mercy of the Prophets. You will attend to that, won't you, Ompar?"

"At once, Kai Winn," he said, clearly quite pleased. Surprisingly, he seemed joyous, even uplifted.

The Kai looked at him. "All things considered, Ompar, you seem to be in good spirits."

"I was thinking we could use this crisis to pull our fractured people together. To refocus their energies in the direction of spirituality and worship." Ompar snorted. "I'm not saying anything is worth the life of innocent Bajorans . . . but if it leads to some degree of cooperation, of unity, perhaps some good will come of this after all."

"I see," said the Kai deliberately. "In other words, you hold with the Terran saying I have heard—about it being necessary to break a few eggs if an omelet is desired."

Ompar shrugged. "Cooking is not my strength, Kai. I will defer to your judgment on that subject."

Winn nodded and indicated with a gesture that he should take his leave—which he did quickly enough. This left the Kai alone with her thoughts.

Ompar's suggestion that the plague was some sort of "punishment" cut far more deeply into her than she would have liked to admit. For Kai Winn carried her own emotional baggage, her own guilt deep within her.

The Kai was supposed to be the personification of the religious purity of Bajor. She felt herself, rightly or wrongly, to be the standard against which all manner of religious matters must be measured.

She had done many things in the pursuit of consolidating her power. They had been done, she felt, for all the right reasons—or so it had seemed at the time. But now those decisions were coming back to haunt her.

Normally, she had utter confidence in what she did. But now she was wondering. She was doubting. She thought in particular about the dealings she had had with the Circle.

But it seemed I'd done the right thing . . .

She thought about her actions in attempting to assassinate Vedek Bareil . . .

But I'd done only what was necessary . . .

Slowly, carefully, Winn began to examine, to scrutinize every action she had taken over her career as Kai. A pattern began to emerge in her mind. It was subtle, but it was there. A pattern, she now began to feel, that suggested selfishness. Power-grabbing. Wrongheadedness.

And was it beyond the realm of possibility that the Prophets were taking her to task for these things? That she had contributed to a sort of deep soul sickness within Bajor? That she had led her people into an abyss from which there might be no escape?

Looking out on the Bajoran countryside, the Kai prayed to the Prophets for guidance.

Unfortunately, if the Prophets heard her supplications, it appeared they were disinclined to provide any sort of response. Unless, of course, one considered death to be a response.

For even as the Kai prayed, Bajorans died—more and more of them all the time.

Captain Benjamin Sisko sat back in his chair, considered the blank monitor screen on his desk, and sighed.

He liked a great many things about his position as commanding officer of *Deep Space Nine*. But there was one thing, above all, that he did not like—and that was the paperwork.

The very term suggested arcane and antiquated

practices, designed to blunt the mind and deaden the soul. Of course, paperwork no longer involved the use of paper, per se. That had gone out with the invention of the computer some four hundred years earlier.

However, the concept of the bureaucracy had managed to survive and Starfleet was as good an example of it as any. And there wasn't anything more bureaucratic in nature than the monthly report.

Of course, that was precisely the thing demanded of Sisko at this moment. If he waited much longer, he would receive a subspace scolding from Starfleet Command.

He sighed again. He would much rather be hitting baseballs in the holodeck, squaring off against some of the greatest pitchers who ever lived.

Unfortunately, the report wasn't going to go away. And he could hardly fault his son Jake for not doing his homework when the captain himself was given to procrastination. So, leaning forward again, he reached for his computer padd—

And heard a familiar feminine voice flood his office. "Sorry to interrupt, Benjamin," said Jadzia Dax over the station's intercom system, "but we've received a vessel from Bajor. I thought you'd want to know, considering it's got one of your favorite people aboard."

Judging from the sarcasm in his friend's voice, Sisko figured it wasn't one of his favorite people at all. And among the Bajorans, there were few people he had an active dislike for.

In fact, there was really only one. He grimaced at the thought.

"Kai Winn," he remarked. It wasn't a question.

"None other," replied Dax, confirming it anyway.

"Did she give any indication as to why she's here?" asked the captain.

"I'm afraid not," the lieutenant told him. "But as always, there's a good chance she's come to see you." There was a pause. "I can stall her if you like. You know, give you time to busy yourself in some obscure part of the station. Maybe take a runabout to the Gamma Quadrant."

Sisko chuckled. "That won't be necessary, Old Man."

It still felt funny to call her that, but she *was* a Trill—a combination of a humanoid host and a vermiform symbiont. It was the symbiont who carried the memories of his friend, Curzon Dax, the "old man" who'd served as its previous host.

"Part of my job," he went on, "is dealing with the Bajoran authorities. And like it or not, Kai Winn is one of those authorities."

"Have it your way," the lieutenant declared. "But if you change your mind, I could arrange an emergency in one of the cargo bays."

The captain smiled to himself. "Thanks, Old Man. I'll keep that in mind."

CHAPTER 3

SISKO FROWNED AND wished he'd taken Dax up on her offer. He'd forgotten how cloyingly sweet the Kai could be when she wanted someone's help. Biting his lip, he considered all she'd told him.

"So this plague," he said out loud, filling his office with his voice, "began with a bunch of replicators?"

"That's the information I've just received," Winn replied calmly. "Mind you, these replicators were not distributed by the government. They were obtained through the most illegal of channels."

"In any case, you're saying that the disease has spread," the captain continued. "Apparently through the water supply, when some of the dying animals polluted it."

She nodded. "Apparently, yes."

"And the whole population is threatened," he concluded.

"That's correct," the Kai replied. "Our immunologists tell us we could face annihilation in a matter of weeks."

She might as well have been talking about the weather in the capitol the day before. However, Sisko sensed an urgency in her that she didn't normally display. The average Bajoran might not have noticed it, but *he* did.

The captain stroked his goatee. "I'm sorry, of course, that this has happened. We'll help in any way we can."

Winn smiled politely. "Good. I knew the Emissary would come to our aid. Otherwise, why would the Prophets have singled you out?"

Sisko shifted in his chair. He'd never been comfortable with the religious identity bestowed on him by the Bajorans.

By all accounts, he'd been the first to communicate with the beings they called the Prophets—the creators of the quadrant's first stable wormhole—and certainly he'd made an interesting first contact. But by his reckoning, he was still just a man.

"Exactly what would you like us to do?" he asked.

The Kai heaved a sigh. "There is so much that needs to be done, I hardly know where to start. Of course, our main goal is to identify the virus and devise a cure. No doubt, your Dr. Bashir has more expertise in such matters than our simple Bajoran scientists."

"Dr. Bashir is a brilliant man," the captain agreed. "Nonetheless, what you're asking for is a tall order, Kai Winn—especially within the time frame you've described."

Winn shrugged. "If it was easy, Emissary, we would have accomplished it ourselves."

Sisko grunted. "Yes, I suppose you would have. Very well, I'll get Bashir working on it. And Dax as well."

"I am grateful," the Kai remarked. "And I am also relieved, because I know you will not fail me."

He looked at her. "The Prophets told you this?"

She returned the look. "Do you have any doubt of it?"

The captain didn't answer her question. He simply said: "We'll do our best. Can I escort you back to your vessel?"

"That won't be necessary," Winn told him. "I know the way." And with that, she got up from her chair and exited his office.

As he watched her go, he felt himself shiver. It was the way he always reacted when he brushed up against something slimy.

Sisko tapped his communications badge, establishing a link with all the other badges on the station. "Major Kira, I need to see you. And bring Odo with you."

"Is there a problem?" asked his first officer.

The captain bit his lip again. "I'm afraid there is," he told her. "I'll fill you in when I see you."

A pause. "We'll be right there," Kira replied.

Sisko shook his head. He wasn't looking forward to telling the major that her whole race was in danger of extinction.

The Bajorans had fought so hard—and endured so much—to throw off the yoke of Cardassian rule. It would be a terrible and ironic shame if they were to succumb to a vicious little bug.

In her office, Kira Nerys studied the pictures of the replicator that Kai Winn had provided. She sifted through them, shaking her head and muttering to herself.

"Something wrong, Major?" came a voice from behind. She turned to see Chief O'Brien behind her. He had a box of tools in his hand.

"Just working on a problem, Chief." Her eyebrows puckered into a question. "And you?"

"You complained your office was too cold last week, remember? I thought I'd check it out for you."

"Oh, right. Fine." She paused a moment and then extended a picture to him. "What's your opinion of this?"

He took the picture and gave it a glance. "Not particularly good composition. It's slightly out of focus, and pardon me for saying so, but it should be more centered . . ."

"I mean of the equipment pictured there, Chief," Kira said patiently.

"Oh." He paused a moment and then shrugged. "Standard replicator model Twenty-One-A. Not exactly state-of-the-art, but a real workhorse. Newer models tend to break down faster. They don't make them like this anymore."

"No one ever makes anything like they did anymore, Chief. At least, that's what I've noticed." She took the picture back and said, "Apparently, it was acquired through the black market."

O'Brien let out a whistle, but then said, "I guess I shouldn't be surprised. You can get anything on the black market, it seems."

"Yes," Kira agreed, "but as near as we can tell, this caused some serious problems. It cooked up some kind of virus that's . . ."

Her voice trailed off as she saw O'Brien's look. That was when she realized and remembered. "By the Prophets—your family's down there."

O'Brien nodded speechlessly and then found his voice. "We've got to get them back up here."

"We can't," Kira told him regretfully. "There's a quarantine on Bajor. No one can come out of there." She hesitated, looking for something to say. "Chief, I wouldn't worry—"

"You wouldn't worry? With all due respect, Major, it's not your wife and daughter down there!"

"No, but it's not as if I don't have friends or family there," Kira said sharply, "and they're Bajoran. So far, it seems we're the only ones affected. To the best of our knowledge, any humans down there are perfectly safe. All right?"

She wasn't sure if he'd even heard her. "Major," he said quickly, "if it's all the same to you . . ."

Kira nodded. "You'd like to adjust my office temperature later, I know. Right now you want to get a call in to your family to make sure they're okay." She waved him off. "Go, go. It's all right. Just get back here before icicles start to form on me."

"Will do," said O'Brien, and he quickly bolted from the room.

Kira sighed. Then she scanned the images of the pictures into the computer. "Computer," she said, "study the images I've just placed into memory and search for any serial numbers or indications of previous ownership."

The computer went to work, and Kira leaned forward, waiting for the results.

Dr. Julian Bashir peered at a series of screens to the left of his research station, where additional clinical data from Bajor was displayed as it was received. He drummed his fingers nervously on his control panel.

Each screen charted a different bio-sign for the population already exhibiting symptoms of the disease. One dealt with respiration, another with heart rate, a third with temperature, and so on. There were details regarding the illness's effect on musculature and nervous system.

The work was remarkably exacting, considering the panic that must have been spreading all over the planet's surface. But then, he reminded himself, the Bajorans were nothing if not dedicated.

Turning to another screen, the doctor regarded the

Bajoran blood sample that had been transported to the station not half an hour ago. Though the sample itself stood under strict quarantine in an electromagnetic construct in the lab next door, Bashir had the feeling it was right in front of him.

An adversary, he thought. And a horrific one at that.

The virus, like all viruses, was basically a helix of DNA. But in this case, it was dark purple and—considering it was without sentience or volition—strangely malevolent-looking, as it floated in a sea of Bajoran blood. While he watched, it invaded a stray skin cell, piercing the cell wall with ease.

The white blood cells that clustered around the entry point did so in vain. They were clearly of no use against the virus.

In a matter of just a few hours, the doctor knew, the invader would force the healthy cell to expend its energies in the creation of another helix—a twin to the first one. And as the first cell collapsed, spent, the second helix would go on to invade a second cell. The process would be repeated, then repeated again, on and on. . . .

Until the host body was so ravaged it couldn't help but succumb. A grisly end, to be sure.

And there was nothing exactly like the virus in his files, which included the sum total of the Federation's medical knowledge. The thing was a stranger, an anomaly.

Bashir turned to Dax, who was sitting at the other

end of the infirmary, charting the spread of the disease across the face of Bajor. Though her back was to him, he could see the results of her work.

Against the greens and browns of Bajor's topography, a number of bright orange lights dotted the map. The greatest cluster was around the Paqu village, where the first outbreak seemed to have occurred. However, as the graphic showed only too well, every continent was now infested with the telltale orange spots.

No surprise there. Bajorans preferred face-to-face contact to electronic communications, so they traveled around their globe more than people on other worlds.

"Jadzia?" he called.

Dax didn't turn around. She just sat there with her back to him.

"Jadzia?" he called again.

Still no answer.

Getting up, the doctor traversed the infirmary and took up a position by the Trill's shoulder. He leaned forward, to get a better look at her.

What he saw took him by surprise. Dax's eyes were red-rimmed, almost welling with tears. And her mouth was a thin hard line.

"Jadzia?" he repeated softly.

Finally her eyes shifted toward his. There was a faraway look to them for a moment. Then they came into focus.

"Julian?" she said. She blinked a few times. "Sorry about that. I guess I wandered off for a second there."

Eyes narrowing with concern, Bashir nodded. "Are you all right?"

The Trill managed a smile. "I'm fine. Just a little tired maybe." She rubbed her eyes.

"You can take a break," he advised her.

Dax shook her head. "No," she said emphatically. "Now where were we?"

"I was about to ask you if you'd seen any changes in the spread of the disease. Pockets of resistance, perhaps."

Returning her attention to the map, she considered it for a moment. Then she gave her response. "No change at all—though I wish I could say otherwise."

The doctor sighed. "I know what you mean."

Dax looked up at him. "How's the culturing going?"

Bashir shrugged. "We won't know for a few hours yet."

He was in the process of producing samples of the virus for testing—a hundred samples, to be exact. Like the original sample he'd received from Bajor, they were in the lab next door.

"In a way," he continued, "it's a good thing that the virus grows so quickly. If it were slower to reproduce, the creation of test samples would have taken a lot longer."

The doctor eyed his friend. "You're sure you're all right?"

Dax dismissed him with a backhanded motion. "Go," she told him. "I'm fine. Really."

He went back to his work, but he could tell there

was something bothering her—distracting her. He didn't have to look far for an explanation, either.

The Trill had always been a compassionate person. And she had made a great many friends among the Bajorans since her arrival on *Deep Space Nine*.

All that misery on the planet had to be affecting her. Ravaging her emotions. Playing havoc with her concentration.

It disturbed him greatly that it should be so. If he was going to come up with a cure for the virus, he would need Dax operating at her best. Her scientific expertise would be invaluable in the hours and days to come.

"Me?" said Quark, working up all the innocence he could.

Odo glared at him from the other side of the polished synthewood bar. He leaned across, so that his face was just inches from the Ferengi's.

"I wouldn't be surprised," the shapeshifter growled.

Quark held his hands out in an appeal for justice— a gesture he'd practiced before a mirror as a boy. "Constable, I had nothing to do with those faulty replicators. And that's the *truth.*"

"You wouldn't know the truth if it walked into your bar and reserved a holosuite." Odo lifted his chin. "And don't call me 'Constable.' I don't like it."

The Ferengi made a show of being hurt. "You like it well enough when Captain Sisko calls you 'Constable'—and I've known you a lot longer than he has. Why, I remember when I first arrived on the station—"

The shapeshifter stopped him with a raised hand. "Don't try to change the subject," he advised. "As you say, I've known you a long time. Now, as I recall, we were talking about replicators—and your involvement with them."

"Or lack thereof," Quark insisted, wagging a peremptory finger. "I'm telling you, this is the first I've heard about it."

"I find that hard to believe," said Odo. "No one's better connected to the black market than you are."

"Nonetheless," the Ferengi told him, "it slipped by me somehow."

He wasn't particularly pleased about it, either. It meant there was new competition out there— competition he hadn't even identified yet.

That was bad. That was *very* bad.

He didn't need to consult the Rules of Acquisition to know he had to do something about it. And quickly, before he lost his reputation as the sector's most resourceful businessman. After all, reputation was everything.

The shapeshifter was scowling, his eyes narrowed as he sized Quark up. "You're not lying about this, are you? Someone really did effect this transaction without your knowing about it."

"That's what I've been trying to tell you." The Ferengi leaned a little closer to Odo. "Just out of curiosity, what are you planning to do about it?"

The shapeshifter's scowl softened a bit. "I'm not quite sure, to be honest. One way or another, it's my job to find out how those replicators made their way to Bajor—and if you're not involved, it's going to make that job a great deal more difficult."

"Especially since there's a new player in the game," Quark remarked.

Odo looked at him. "In other words, if it was one of the usual suspects, you would have known about it."

The Ferengi shrugged. "Something like that."

The shapeshifter grunted. "Well, if you hear anything, I trust you'll let me know."

"I will indeed," Quark assured him.

With a last wary glance over his shoulder, Odo threaded his way past the paying customers and out of the bar. As the Ferengi watched him go, determination took hold of him.

After all, it was in his own interest to find out who had dealt those replicators to Bajor. He vowed to expose the unprincipled swine who was muscling in on his territory, one way or the other.

"Not the replicators?" Sisko echoed.

"That's correct," said Dr. Bashir. He looked at the others assembled in the captain's office—specifically, Dax, Kira, Odo, and O'Brien. "I was leary of that conclusion as soon as I heard it. After all, replicators can't create stable lifeforms—not even on the cellular level, to my knowledge."

"Then where did the virus come from?" inquired Odo.

"Good question," said the doctor. He held up a

medical tricorder. "I had the opportunity to analyze a sample of the raw matter supply that came with the replicators—using an electromagnetic shield, of course, to prevent contamination of the station." He frowned as he turned to Sisko. "Apparently, it was the matter itself that carried the virus."

The captain took the tricorder and went over the data displayed on it. "I don't get it," he replied. "Are you saying that whoever gave Paqu village the replicators . . . *wanted* to inflict a virus on Bajor?"

Bashir shook his head from side to side. "I don't think so. More likely, the virus was dormant and undetectable, even to the smugglers. They probably had no idea what they were carrying."

"And then the replication process woke the buggers up," O'Brien suggested. "Is that what you're saying, Doctor?"

Bashir nodded. "That's what I'm saying, Chief. If the raw matter had been subjected to a Federation-level inspection, the virus would have been detected and the population could have been protected from it. But seeing as how smugglers don't bother with such details. . . ."

His voice trailed off ominously. Not that he had to finish—judging from everyone's expressions, they all got the picture.

"What about a vaccine?" asked Dax. "Are they having any luck?"

"No more than before," the doctor informed her. "Basically, they're tinkering with broad-based vaccines that have proven effective elsewhere. But this virus has so far resisted everything they've thrown at it."

"Have they continued with . . . quarantines?" Kira suggested, her voice quavering ever so slightly.

"Already in place," said Bashir, albeit reluctantly. "In Paqu village and wherever else there's been a concentration of cases." He gazed sympathetically at the Bajoran. "I'm sorry, Major. I know the thought of your people penned up like lab subjects cannot be a pleasant one."

"To say the least," breathed Kira, suddenly finding something interesting to look at on the bulkhead.

Obviously, thought Sisko, she was taking this thing pretty hard. And why not? This wasn't some race she'd had to think of only in the abstract. The Bajorans were her people. They were her *blood*.

"Maybe if we knew where the virus came from," O'Brien proposed, "we'd have a better idea of how to deal with it."

"Good idea," the doctor confirmed. "As a matter of fact, Jadzia's already done some work along those lines."

Dax nodded. "The theory was that if we traced the raw matter trail far enough back, we might find someone who's come up with a cure for the virus—or at least a way to slow the spread of it. Or, failing that, we might gain some insight into the type of environment it grew up in—so we can experiment with its reaction to adverse conditions."

"And?" the captain prompted.

"I matched up the observed symptoms with those recorded in the computer's medical logs," the Trill explained.

"Don't tell me the Cardassians had a hand in this," O'Brien interjected. His brow creased. "Or worse yet, the Dominion . . ."

Odo frowned at the suggestion. He was obviously uncomfortable with the fact that his people, the Dominion's "founders," were perhaps the biggest threat to the Federation in its history.

"No," Dax responded. "Nothing like that. As it happens, this particular set of symptoms has shown up in four sectors of space. Two were within the Federation, one in the Gorn Hegemony, and one in Orion space."

"One of the instances in the Federation was on Vulcan," Bashir told them. "But we can rule that one out, since Vulcan blood is so different from the Bajoran variety. The other instance was on Cabrius Prime—but we can eliminate that one as well."

"Why is that?" asked Kira.

The doctor smiled grimly. "Cabrius Prime was destroyed in a supernova some thirty-five years ago. There's no life there, viral or otherwise."

The major grunted. "Sorry I asked."

"What about the other two possibilities?" Sisko asked.

"The Gorn case," said the Trill, "turned out to be a dead end as well. It seems their problem wasn't a virus at all, but a subtle form of radiation poisoning. When they eliminated the radiation leak, the symptoms went away."

"That leaves the Orions," observed Odo.

Bashir nodded. "So it does. I'd say there's a good chance that's where the virus came from. Especially when you consider the Orions' predilection for smuggling and other illegal ventures."

"But the Orions aren't a single unified population," Sisko reminded them. "They're spread out into several large factions and a great many smaller ones, separated by space and allegiances and cultural differences. In short, knowing the Orions are the culprits only gives us a starting point."

"In other words," said Kira, "we need to know *which* Orions."

"That's right," the captain agreed. "And there are only two ways to find that out. One is to try to determine who on Bajor has ever dealt with Orions—or might have considered it." He looked to his first officer.

"I'm on it," Kira assured him.

"So am I," said Odo.

"And the other way?" asked Dax.

"The other way," said Sisko, "is one we'll hold in abeyance—in case the first way doesn't work."

CHAPTER
4

"NOTHING?" SISKO LOOKED across his desk at Kira and couldn't quite keep the astonishment out of his voice. "You've found nothing to link anyone on Bajor with the Orions?"

Kira nodded reluctantly. "Look, sir, I'm no innocent when it comes to the black market. In fact, I'm as well-connected as anyone. When we were fighting the Cardassians, we had to be. It was the only way we could get the weapons we needed." She paused. "So if I haven't come up with anything—"

Sisko held up a hand for peace. "I'm not implying that you're giving less than your best effort, Major. I'm just a bit . . . surprised. Usually you're quite tenacious when it comes to getting information. For you to admit defeat . . ."

"I haven't admitted any such thing," bristled Kira, "and I certainly hope you don't think you need to give me some sort of reverse-psychology prodding."

"Never even occurred to me," Sisko replied mildly.

"This isn't over yet," she assured him, "not by a long shot. If there's a connection, I'll find it. But whoever we're dealing with is damned good. Odo and I tracked the serial numbers through about five levels of supply, down to a parts wholesaler called Starway Equipment Supplies. A wholesaler which has since . . ."

"Let me guess," said Sisko. "Disappeared."

"Exactly," Kira confirmed. "Disappeared, if it ever existed in the first place. Probably called themselves something else the week before, and something else again the week after. So we're going to approach this from a different angle."

He was interested. "That being—?"

The major frowned. "I'm not sure yet. There are several possibilities, none of which I'm particularly—"

That was when the proximity alarm began to shriek.

Sisko and Kira were immediately on their feet. "Report!" the captain called out as he made his way to the door.

"Ship approaching, Benjamin," Dax said from her station. "It hasn't offered any hails and it's ignoring ours."

"Did it come through the wormhole?" he asked, descending into Ops.

"Negative," Dax said.

"Let's see it," Sisko said. A moment later, the ship in question flickered into existence. He recognized it immediately. "It's Maquis," he noted.

"Definitely," Kira said, not waiting for Dax to answer.

"Still no answer to our hail," the Trill reported.

"Put me on," Sisko commanded.

Dax opened up a frequency and nodded to Sisko that all was ready for him to speak. The ship loomed larger on their screen as the captain extended a warning.

"Maquis ship, this is Captain Benjamin Sisko. You have not been cleared for approach. If you do not respond immediately, we will assume you to be hostile and act accordingly."

There was a moment of silence as Sisko's threat hung in the air. There was not a single doubt in the mind of anyone in the room that he would do exactly as he promised.

Abruptly, a female voice crackled back over the ether. "That will not be necessary, Captain. I am alone in this vessel and have no intention of launching any sort of attack on your station."

Sisko frowned. "Identify yourself."

"We're getting a visual transmission," Dax said.

"On screen," the captain told her.

The image of the Maquis ship rippled and was replaced by the face of a determined-looking Bajoran. Kira blinked in surprise.

"I am Ro Laren," the Bajoran said. And with more

than a touch of irony, she added, "Perhaps you've heard of me."

"The former Starfleet lieutenant who was given a second chance, and threw that chance back at Starfleet in order to join the terrorist group called the Maquis. Yes, I believe we have a passing familiarity with you," Sisko said dryly.

Ro smiled thinly. "As dazzled as I am by your rapier wit, Captain, I'd appreciate it if you could sheathe it for the moment."

Sisko glanced at Dax. In a soft voice, he said, "Keep monitoring her weapons systems, make sure she doesn't power them up." Then he turned back to the screen to face Ro. "Are you here to turn yourself in?" he asked.

She grunted. "Not exactly. I'm here under a flag of truce."

"Not to quibble over a fine point," Sisko replied, "but you're a criminal, wanted for crimes by Starfleet. It may not be within my power to grant you any sort of truce. I could be accused of aiding and abetting a known felon."

"True enough," Ro said. "I should point out a couple of things. One, please note that I've halted my vehicle at a distance out of range of your station, so I pose no immediate threat."

Sisko glanced at Dax, who nodded in confirmation.

Ro went on. "This means that at the moment I cannot hurt you. By the same token, you can't hurt me. I could keep this up all day, as could you, but that would be a waste of our time. If you refuse to cooperate, hear me out, or provide me a path of safe passage, then I will simply turn around and be on my way."

"Rendering this a pointless exercise," Sisko observed.

"Correct. But if I do that, then you can explain to the Bajoran government that help for a planet in the grip of an epidemic was turned away by one Captain Benjamin Sisko, simply because he didn't want to take the chance of treading on any Starfleet toes."

"What sort of 'help' are you talking about?" asked the captain.

"I'm talking supplies," Ro said. "I'm talking food and medicine, untainted. You're welcome to check it out yourselves if you don't believe me, although why I would want to sicken a planet that's already ailing is beyond me.

"Look, Captain, once upon a time, I joined Starfleet. Then I joined the Maquis. Ultimately, it doesn't matter if I paint my face white and join the circus. I am, first and foremost, Bajoran, and I could not find it within myself to abandon my people.

"Even though it meant bumping heads with my Maquis brethren, and they've got some of the hardest heads I've ever seen. Even though it meant fighting to draw supplies from our own stock, which is not exactly copious. Even though it meant . . ." She paused and then shrugged. "Never mind what it meant. The bottom line is I'm here to help. And I'll be happy to jump through whatever hoops you want to hold up so I can do that."

Sisko grunted at the image on the monitor. Lieutenant Ro Laren, the Maquis's most infamous defector. Here. Now. Asking to help out in the fight against the disease ravaging Bajor.

This was about the *last* thing he'd expected.

Beside him, Kira chuckled dryly. "If the Federation knew they could have drawn out the Maquis so easily . . ."

"Yes," Dax chimed in humorlessly. "And all it took was a deadly plague."

The captain ignored their comments, concentrating on Ro. The woman looked sincere enough, but looks could be deceiving.

Of course, it was possible the former Starfleet officer had had a pang of conscience, as she claimed. But he couldn't rule out the possibility that this was some kind of Maquis trick—an attempt to breach the station's defenses, perhaps, and take over control of the wormhole.

After all, it had worked for the Greeks at the walls of Troy. And what could be more innocent than a vessel carrying food and medical supplies?

Sisko leaned closer to the monitor. "I hate to bring this up," he said, "but you're wanted for desertion and treason, Lieutenant. I think I'm going to have to pass on your offer."

Ro leaned forward on her end as well. "Then you're a fool, Captain. And so am I, I guess, because everything I've heard about you is wrong."

Sisko winced. "I appreciate the compliment, Lieutenant—lefthanded though it may be—but it doesn't change my mind. You're a security risk. Plague or no plague, I can't let you set foot on this station."

The Maquis bit her lip. "All right, then," she told him. "I won't set foot on the station. If you want, you can beam over here. Or if that's not good enough, we can continue to speak the way we're speaking now. I just want to do my part to help my people."

Kira made a derisive sound deep in her throat. "Oh? Then where's she been for the past several years?"

Ro's features went taut. "I beg your pardon, Major?"

Kira hadn't intended for her remark to be heard, but she didn't back down. Quite the contrary, in fact.

"I was wondering," she expanded, "why you weren't here when Bajor *really* needed your help. You know, when we were fighting the Cardassians? Or afterward, when we were trying to salvage a civilization from what little they'd left us?"

Damn, thought Sisko. Why did the communications system have to pick *now* to work so well?

"Let's keep our personal feelings out of this," he said pointedly, glancing at Kira. Then, returning his attention to Ro, he added, "I still don't see why I should take such a risk, Lieutenant. So—"

"Wait," the deserter blurted. "Please." Her face seemed racked with pain. "Look, I know I'm not going to win any popularity contests—not with the Bajorans and not with Starfleet."

"That's for sure," whispered O'Brien, careful to remain offscreen and out of earshot.

"But I can help you in ways other people can't," Ro insisted. "I'm not just talking about food and medicine. I'm talking about expertise. About connections in the black market." Her brow creased. "You speak of risk, Captain. What kind of risk are you taking by *not* allowing me to help?"

Sisko sighed. The woman had a point there.

Ro had been through Starfleet's advanced tactical training course, which made her a considerable asset when it came to undercover work. Add to that her familiarity with the black market, on which the Maquis depended almost daily, and she presented an almost irresistible package—at a time when Bajor needed all the help it could get.

The captain could feel the glare of Kira's scrutiny. "Please tell me you're not going to do this," she said.

Still attending to the monitor, Sisko drew a long breath, then let it out. An idea was forming in his head—an idea his first officer wouldn't like very much.

In fact, she would hate it. But she would also see the wisdom in it. At least, he hoped she would.

"Drop your shields," he told Ro. "We're coming aboard."

The Maquis looked at him with narrowed eyes—though she'd invited him to board her vessel just a few moments ago. *"We,* Captain?"

Sisko nodded. "Major Kira and I. We've got a mission to discuss."

Kira turned to him, eyes wide. Her expression was that of someone who had been betrayed, and betrayed badly.

He tried not to look at her too much as he made his way to the transporter unit.

Odo tilted his head. "Are you absolutely certain about this, Captain?"

Sisko, who was sitting behind the desk in his office, shrugged and picked up the baseball that had become a permanent fixture there. He turned it in his hand, considering its seamed surface.

"Listen," he said, as if to the ball, "I don't like the idea of dealing with the Orions any more than you do. But let's face it. If those replicators arrived courtesy of an Orion trader, we've got to find out who it is. And we haven't been able to do that by investigating the Bajorans."

The shapeshifter grunted. "Hard to argue with your logic," he conceded. "But even if we get in touch with the right parties, they're not going to be eager to tell you anything. There may not be honor among thieves, but there is a common fear of reprisal. If one Orion spills the beans about another Orion, he can pretty much bet the favor will be returned someday."

The captain looked up. "In other words," he remarked, "it'll be difficult to get anything out of them."

"In other words," Odo replied, "it'll be *very* difficult."

Sisko smiled. "Under normal circumstances, I'd agree. The trick is to bring in another element. Say, someone who can spill the beans about them just as thoroughly as their fellow thieves. Better, maybe." His smile widened. "And that's where *you* come in."

The shapeshifter couldn't conceal his surprise. "Me?" he repeated lamely.

"That's right," the captain told him. "After all, who's better connected in this sector? Who knows more about the Orions than they know about themselves?"

Odo shook his head. "I'm sorry," he said. "While all that is true, I am definitely *not* the best man for the job."

Sisko's smile slowly vanished. "And why not?" he demanded.

"Because," the shapeshifter responded in measured tones, "I have never met an Orion. In fact, I've never even seen one."

The captain's brow creased. "But I thought—"

"And it was not an unreasonable conclusion," Odo interjected, anticipating the rest of the man's statement. "But the fact remains—everything I know about Orions, I've gleaned from second-hand sources."

Sisko frowned. He looked as if he would have liked to pursue the matter, but there was really nothing left to pursue.

"In that case," he said wistfully, "I'm sorry to have bothered you, Constable."

Odo watched the human toss the ball up and snatch it out of the air—an outward sign of his frustration.

Captain Sisko was not the kind of man to give vent to his anger. It was only in small gestures that he demonstrated his emotions.

Too bad, thought Odo. He liked Sisko. He respected him for what he had accomplished here. What's more, the captain had always treated him fairly.

Odo wished he could have helped in this Orion gambit, especially considering its implications for the future of Bajor. However . . .

Suddenly it came to him. Maybe *he* couldn't help, but there was someone else who *could*. Someone, in fact, on this very station.

He cleared his throat, causing Sisko to look up at him. "If I may make a suggestion . . ." the security chief began.

Quark inspected the faint blue drop of dried g'nerra juice that marred the otherwise spotless surface of his bar. With an expression of disgust, he glanced at his brother Rom, who was cheerfully completing his daily cleaning chores at the bar's opposite end.

Taking out a pluffa sponge from underneath the bar, Quark went to work on the g'nerra drop. Little by little, it rubbed off. But, thought the Ferengi, as he put the sponge away again, he didn't have time to tidy up the place. That's what his brother was for.

Sighing, Quark recalled the sixth rule of acquisition: "Never allow family to stand in the way of opportunity."

It was a good rule. It was an outstanding rule. Yet

he continued to disregard it, day in and day out, by keeping Rom in his employ.

And why? Because his brother would have been an even bigger pain in the lobes if he were working somewhere else, where Quark couldn't keep an eye on him.

His reverie was interrupted by the approach of a customer. At least, the Ferengi *thought* it was a customer—until he saw the black beard that went with the man's red-and-black Starfleet uniform.

"Captain Sisko," he said, mustering up all the considerable charm at his disposal. "To what do I owe the pleasure?"

Unfortunately, pleasure would have nothing to do with it. Quark knew from sad experience that when the captain approached the bar, he had a bone to pick. It was just a question of which bone it would be.

The Ferengi bit his lip. Not that little oversight concerning the regulator nodes, he hoped. That had been the Maratekkan's fault more than his. And besides, how was *he* supposed to know the damned things had gotten polarized in the blasted storage compartment?

"Actually," Sisko said, as he pulled up a seat at the bar, "there's something I'd like to discuss with you." And then it happened. The captain *smiled* at him.

Quark shook his head, not at all sure what to make of that. Then he noticed that something else was wrong as well.

"You're sitting at the bar," he observed. He looked

at Sisko with a wary eye. "You *never* sit at the bar. You always take a *table.*"

"Well," the human countered, "I guess there's a first time for everything."

The Ferengi swallowed. There was something going on here, something that was going to leap up and bite him where he sat if he wasn't careful. But what was it?

What in the name of the Nagus did Sisko have in mind?

"Can I . . . er, get you a drink?" he offered, stalling for time. "On the house, of course."

The captain thought about it for a moment. "How about a glass of wine? Something red, not too sweet."

Alarms went off in Quark's head. Sisko *never* ordered wine. He always had a raktajino. As the Ferengi reached under the bar for the Terran vintage Bashir favored, his mind was racing.

However, for the life of him, he couldn't figure out what the captain wanted. Not as he grabbed a glass, or as he poured, or as he placed the wine glass on the bar His only option, he realized, was the one he hated most of all.

He would just have to wait and see.

In no apparent hurry, Sisko raised the glass and took a sip. He smiled again, forcing a little shudder out of Quark.

"Perfect," he said. "Just what I had in mind." He leaned closer to the bar. "You know," he added, "you're a hell of a bartender."

That did it, thought the Ferengi. A smile, he could tolerate. A seat at the bar, even a sudden yen for the fruit of the grapevine. But a *compliment?* From Benjamin *Sisko?*

"All right," he blurted, "what is it? What do you want from me? Just tell me and get it over with." He drew a ragged breath. "I can't stand the suspense."

The human swirled the wine in his glass. "It's nothing much, really. Just that I hear you're something of an expert on the Orions."

Quark looked at him. "The Orions?" he repeated.

"Uh-huh." Sisko held his drink up appraisingly to the light. "I have it on good authority that you completed a rather complex negotiation with them recently. In the matter of some slave women, I believe."

The Ferengi held up his hands. "That was perfectly legitimate," he maintained.

"Oh?" Sisko said, peering over the rim of his glass.

"Absolutely," Quark insisted. "Of course, I might have *bent* a few regulations to bring those poor abused females to civilized space—but they were *Orion* regulations. As far as the Federation is concerned, everything I did was according to the book."

"I see," the captain replied. "And what exactly did you have in mind for these poor abused females— now that you own them?"

The Ferengi winced. *"Own* is such a harsh word. I prefer to think of them as individuals, free and enfranchised—who happen to owe me a debt of gratitude. And if they choose to display that gratitude by working as dabo girls in my establishment?" He shrugged. "Who am I to deprive them of their dignity?"

Sisko looked around at the rather sparse lunchtime crowd. "And with Orions as dabo girls, you're certain to pack the place. Aren't you?"

Quark smiled. "Sometimes," he explained, "good deeds are rewarded. This may turn out to be one of those times."

"Then there was nothing about the transaction I need to have investigated?" the human asked.

"Nothing at all," the Ferengi assured him.

Apparently, he told himself, his fears had been unfounded. Inwardly, he heaved a sigh of relief.

"Now," he continued, "if you'll excuse me, I have—"

"Just a minute," Sisko said.

Quark frowned. He knew it was too good to be true.

"Yes?" he responded.

The human took another sip of his wine and replaced his glass on the table. "I need a favor from you," he declared.

The Ferengi looked at him. "What kind of favor?"

Sisko's demeanor changed. Suddenly he looked a lot more grim.

"A big favor," he replied.

Quark felt faint. "How big?"

"Very big," the human told him.

Then Sisko told him about how they had narrowed down the suppliers of the replicators to the Orions. And he described what he wanted of the Ferengi.

Quark hadn't had any luck with his own investigation, so he was glad to learn that someone else had. But that wasn't the only reason he felt a smile spreading across his face. In fact, by the time the captain was finished asking his favor, Quark was positively euphoric.

"You don't look as distressed as I thought you would," Sisko observed. "Just why is that?"

That's when the Ferengi told him about Mephil Trantos.

CHAPTER
5

O'BRIEN STOOD AT his console in Ops and watched the *Defiant* describe a tight arc in space. A moment later, it switched from thrusters to impulse engines and took off.

"*Defiant* has left the station and is on course," he announced.

"Acknowledged," Dax replied a little absently.

She was at her customary station as well—at least in body. Her mind, O'Brien decided, was somewhere else, and had been since she set foot in Ops a little while ago.

No doubt, she was worried about the disease down on Bajor. But then, they all were—O'Brien as well.

He couldn't help remembering that Keiko and Molly were on the planet's surface—trapped, now

73

that a quarantine was in place, though the disease seemed only to effect the Bajorans. With communications channels between *Deep Space Nine* and Bajor devoted almost exclusively to the exchange of medical data, the chief had only been able to talk to his wife once.

Keiko had told him that no one on their island had been afflicted with the disease—at least, not yet. They were continuing their work, waiting for word that it would be safe to leave.

Apparently, Molly had been unruffled by the heightened tension among the adults. Though she sensed something was wrong, Keiko had said, there was no fear in her.

O'Brien smiled now at the image. *Stay that way, both of you,* he urged them silently. *We'll get you out of this before too long.*

A voice broke into his thoughts.

"We're receiving a communication from Starfleet Command," announced Ensign Michael Hagen, a short dark-haired man who'd arrived with the latest batch of fleet personnel. He looked to the Trill, who'd been left in charge of the station. "They're asking for Captain Sisko, sir."

Dax didn't seem to hear him.

Hagen spoke a little louder. "It's Starfleet Command, Lieutenant. Should I put them through on your monitor?"

Emerging from some private reverie, the Trill seemed a little disoriented as she responded. "By all means, Mr. Hagen, put them through."

Watching Dax from Kira's station, O'Brien frowned. He'd served under all kinds of commanding officers, from the stubborn and later fanatical Ben Maxwell to the sure and even-handed Jean-Luc Picard to the dedicated and occasionally fiery Benjamin Sisko.

All were strong figures who commanded respect, no matter their idiosyncrasies. Dax, of course, seemed far more interested in her research and her studies than in the exigencies of command. Yet, thanks to the memories she carried from her past host bodies, she was capable of leading when the situation called for it.

At least, that would normally have been the case. Right now, O'Brien thought, she was letting her preoccupation get the better of her.

Her conversation with Starfleet seemed to come to an end rather quickly. Dax shook her head in annoyance.

He made his way over to her. "Problem, Lieutenant?"

The Trill glanced at him. "Not really, Chief. Command was just looking for an update on the plague." Her brow creased for a moment, as if she were in some kind of pain, then it smoothed over again. "I wish I had more to tell them," she added. "All I could say was that Julian is doing his best."

O'Brien nodded. "I checked the perimeter sensors. You'll be glad to hear there's no sign of the Cardassians."

One fear he had harbored was that with the sector

critical, the Cardassians would move in and cause trouble. So far, that didn't seem to be the case.

Dax sighed. "That's good to hear. Thanks, Chief."

"Don't mention it," O'Brien replied.

He had started back to his post when someone called him. It was Hagen. The chief joined the new man at his console,

"What can I do for you?" he asked.

Hagen looked uncomfortable. "Sir," he said in a quiet voice, "three requests for departure from the station have been filed in the last twenty minutes or so. They're queued on Lieutenant Dax's line, but she's not acting on them." He winced. "We're getting some rather irate protests from the ships' captains."

O'Brien nodded. "Good lad," he replied. "I'll handle it."

Completing the journey to his console, he accessed Dax's comm line and confirmed the information he'd been given. It was true, apparently. Three requests for departure had indeed piled up over the last twenty minutes, and not one had received a reply.

The chief scowled. It was understandable that Dax should be worried about the Bajorans. It was *not* understandable that she was ignoring her responsibilities as acting commander.

Crossing Ops again, he moved to the Trill's side. "Lieutenant," he asked, "is there some problem with the departure requests?"

Dax looked at O'Brien, her eyes wider than usual. "What do you mean?"

He pointed to her screen and showed her. Along the

right-hand side, there was a list of ships waiting to depart.

The Trill frowned. "Damn. I should have seen that."

She began to assess each request and issue curt orders. In a matter of minutes, she had everything sorted out.

Another crisis averted, O'Brien mused. But he'd barely finished the thought when Hagen came to him with something else, a new expression of concern on his face.

"Sir?" said the specialist.

"Go ahead," O'Brien told him.

"We have a problem with the ventilation subroutines," Hagen reported. "I'm reading some power fluctuations—"

"I fixed them," the chief pointed out, with more than a little annoyance. And he had—shortly after Keiko's departure.

The specialist nodded. "I know, sir. But they're back again."

The chief grunted. "Acknowledged, Mr. Hagen. I'll look into it."

It was the third programming problem caused by the spikes. O'Brien had to wonder if he was missing something.

Below Ops, in the infirmary, Bashir was in the midst of congratulating himself. The monitor in front of him showed him a microscopic swarm of bent DNA helixes—concrete evidence of his triumph.

He had done it. He had discovered a cure for the virus.

Taking a cue from the proteins it contained, he had ordered a vast collection of serums from the medical database. It helped that he could discount several hundred serums already tested by the Bajoran doctors.

Still, with millions of possibilities to sift through, he had needed to isolate the ones most likely to destroy the invading disease. His hunch about the proteins had done that.

The result? A single serum that encouraged the virus to create flawed copies of itself—copies incapable of replicating themselves. And if the virus couldn't replicate, it would be gone in a single generation.

The doctor smiled as he checked and rechecked the results of the one successful test. There had been no mistakes. He had really done it.

End of disease, end of threat, end of story.

Tapping his communicator badge, he put in a call to Ops. "Bashir to Dax."

There was a delay, perhaps longer than there should have been. "Dax here. What is it, Julian?"

"Good news," he told her. "I've got a cure."

There was a pause on the other end, as of disbelief. "That's wonderful," said the Trill.

Yes, he couldn't help thinking, it *is* pretty wonderful, isn't it? But what he said was "I couldn't have done it without the Bajorans. I've got to tell them about it as quickly as—"

The doctor stopped in midsentence as he caught sight of something on the monitor in front of him— something that filled him with cold crawling terror. Where only moments ago there had been a swarm of bent helixes, they were now being joined by an army of healthy ones—helixes every bit as capable of multiplying as their forebears had been.

Bashir shook his head. He had never seen anything like it. Somehow, in a matter of minutes, the virus had mutated into something impervious to his cure. It was back in business again.

And the Bajorans were just as badly off as before. Even worse, perhaps, since there was now one less thing that could stop the plague.

"Julian?" Dax said. "I didn't catch the rest of what you were saying."

The doctor swallowed his bitter pill. "I was wrong, Jadzia. It's not the cure I thought it was. In fact," he told her, with infinite disappointment, "we're back to square one."

Again, there was a pause on the other end. "I'm sorry," his friend said, an emptiness in her voice that made it clear her comment was an understatement. In fact, she was very, *very* sorry his cure hadn't worked.

"So am I," he said. "So am I."

"You've got to keep trying," she told him. "Those people down there . . ." Her voice trailed off.

"I know," he told her. "Bashir out."

Leaning back in his chair, heavy with frustration, he eyed the army of helixes once more. *Damn*, he thought. The thing was spreading with every passing moment, and he hadn't done a thing about it.

Yet, he reminded himself—and got back to work.

Kira had made up her mind that she simply wasn't going to speak to Ro. That's all. She wasn't going to speak to her.

Oh, sure, she might say something along the lines of "Watch out, that boulder is falling on you!" Something like that. Otherwise, though, she was just going to keep to herself.

She had figured that she would get some measure of satisfaction from that. But as they trudged across the rough terrain ahead of them, Kira discovered something interesting—namely, that it wasn't particularly fulfilling giving someone the silent treatment when that person's demeanor and manner made it clear she couldn't care less.

To make matters worse, Ro was whistling.

And to make matters even worse than that, she was whistling off-key.

Their field packs jostled against their backs as Ro contentedly rendered some tune Kira couldn't even begin to identify. Just when Ro reached the end of it and relief seemed in sight, she started all over again.

They were climbing a small incline studded with tufts of grass. Kira remembered this area from her youth; it had been a favorite hiding place of those trying to stay one step ahead of the Cardassians.

There were plenty of places in which to hide, and

the terrain was uneven. Of course, she was fit enough to handle that with no problem.

Secretly, she kept waiting for Ro to have some sort of difficulty keeping up. But no, the Maquis just kept whistling and eating ground at a steady, even pace.

Kira, meanwhile, found herself starting to get a bit parched. She tried not to acknowledge it for as long as she could, but the Bajoran sun seemed particularly hot that day, and finally the major decided to take a break.

She didn't announce her intention. She simply dropped herself down by the nearest reasonably shady tree.

Ro's whistling never wavered, not even to acknowledge the sudden stop. Most irritating of all, she didn't sit down. She simply leaned against the tree, arms folded, and continued chirping that same damned song.

Kira took a quick drink from her carefully rationed water and tried, tried with all her willpower, not to say anything. But finally she couldn't stand it anymore.

"Would you please stop that damned whistling?" she said.

It promptly ceased.

To be immediately replaced by a humming.

Kira softly thudded her head against the tree. "You're doing this deliberately to irritate me, aren't you?"

"No," Ro said. "I'm doing it to amuse myself. Irritating you is just a side benefit."

"Well," Kira rejoined, "I hope you're amused."

Ro glanced at her. "Actually, it's hard to determine what's more amusing—your irritation or your holier-than-thou attitude."

"My attitude?" Kira snorted derisively. "You Maquis . . . the lot of you . . . acting as if you're the moral conscience of the galaxy. . . ."

"We don't act that way at all, Major," Ro retorted. "We simply act like people who want what is, by all rights, ours. That doesn't seem particularly unreasonable to me. You remember what that's like, don't you? Back in the days when the cry was 'Bajor for Bajorans?' A cry that's been replaced by, 'We've got ours and you're on your own.'"

"The situations aren't comparable," Kira shot back. "We were rallying against a tyrant. You're trying to destroy a treaty." She thought about Bereil and what he had died for. "An *important* treaty."

"So treaties make the difference," Ro said. "I see. And if some sort of puppet Bajoran government had officially signed an agreement with the Cardassians forty years ago, happily turning Bajor over to them, why then everything would have been different. You'd never have rebelled, never fought back. You'd have smiled, bobbed your head, and accepted what was given to you. Is that what you're telling me?"

"I'm telling you that that was then, and this is now," Kira insisted.

Ro shook her head, and now she, too, finally sat. But it was on the opposite side of the tree from Kira, her back likewise against the trunk. "You know . . . I think about what we were once, and what we've now become. And I wonder if maybe we don't deserve this disease."

Kira had been determined not to make any accusations, warranted as they were. But she couldn't stop herself anymore.

"If you believe all that," she said, glancing over her shoulder, "then why the hell did you come back? Especially since you didn't have any problem abandoning Bajor before."

Ro looked at her. "I didn't abandon Bajor. I joined Starfleet."

"Because you couldn't stand to watch what was happening here?"

The muscles in Ro's jaw fluttered. "All right. If you like. I couldn't watch us act like sheep, always turning the other cheek."

"Not all of us did that," Kira told her. "But then, you had to be here to see that."

The time, Ro didn't reply.

Kira shook her head and got to her feet. "Come on. Let's go."

Ro did as she was bade, dusting off her trousers. She followed Kira with quick, steady strides.

"So where is this latest contact of yours?" the Maquis asked.

"Just over the next rise. And you don't have to sound so sarcastic with that 'latest' comment."

"Oh, well," Ro said, "pardon my sarcasm. It's simply that, so far, we've been through two large cities and checked through all sorts of underground haunts, with you claiming the entire time that you know who to talk to, where to talk to them, and just what to say to get the information we need. And every place we've looked, your beloved contacts are either dead or ignorant. And in at least one case, both."

"I have confidence in Comvic Cam," Kira said flatly. "We should have gone to him in the first place. He fought at my side when we were in the Shakaar cel."

"Ah, yes, the Shakaar cel. Back in the days when it was acceptable to be a rebel."

"Drop dead," Kira said.

"I've no immediate plans to do so," Ro told her, "but I'm sure the plague will do what it can."

And she started to whistle once more.

Comvic Cam's home was nothing extraordinary. A simple one-room cabin situated on the top of a hill, surrounded by a particularly dense patch of forest.

As they made their way through, Ro muttered, "So let me get this straight. This guy, who lives in the middle of nowhere, away from everything . . . you're saying he's so completely a part of everything that he's going to be able to guide us to the origins of the virus? Maybe even steer us toward a cure?"

"You don't have to be in the center of town to stay up on current events," Kira explained. "Comvic has a large number of friends and a very long reach. He knows what's going on."

Ro grunted. "I believe this is where you're supposed to say, 'Trust me.'"

"I figure it would be better for both of us if I didn't waste my breath."

"That's the smartest thing I've heard you say yet."

Kira turned to her, her hands on her hips. "Look, Ro, I want you to promise me something."

"The promise of a traitor and a Maquis? What's that worth, I wonder?"

"Probably not much, but I'm asking anyway. Comvic is an old friend, even though I haven't seen him in many years. I want you to treat him with the proper respect."

Ro studied her a moment, stroking her chin. "You really think of me as some sort of loose cannon, don't you? Ready to shoot my mouth off, do whatever I want and damn the consequences?"

"I'd say that's a fair assessment, yes."

"So tell me, 'former rebel' . . . how did they see you when you first came aboard *Deep Space Nine?*"

With no trace of irony, Kira said, "As a professional."

"Well, I'm a professional, too. I guess you just don't like what I'm good at."

"Just promise me—"

"Fine, fine, I promise," Ro said impatiently.

"And leave everything to me," Kira advised her.

"Done."

"Don't try to help me."

"Am I not making myself sufficiently clear?" Ro asked. "You take the lead, Major. You be in charge, you satisfy your ego and your desire to run the show.

I'll be right behind you, applauding your every move."

Kira shook her head. "You're impossible," she said.

The trail had brought them within range of the house, and they headed toward it. Ro turned to Kira.

"Are you sure he's still there, Major?"

In point of fact, Kira wasn't sure at all. This was simply the last place where she'd known Comvic to be living. But with utter confidence, she said, "Absolutely."

Then she walked up to the door and the ground crumbled beneath her—dropping her into a dark dank pit. She was lucky she hadn't twisted an ankle in the process.

Ro came forward to look down at her over the edge of the pit. "Problem, Major?" she asked.

Kira snarled at her. "Of course there's a problem. What are you, blind? I'm in a pit, for crying out loud!"

"Yes, so I see," Ro observed thoughtfully.

There was a moment of silence. "Well?" Kira shouted.

"I don't know," said the Maquis. "It *could* be a well, I suppose, although I didn't hear a splash. There doesn't seem to be much in the way of wat—"

Kira fumed. "Not 'well' as in 'Is this a well?' 'Well' as in 'Well, what are you going to do to get me out of here?'"

Ro folded her arms across her chest. "You know, as I recall, someone said to leave everything to them.

'Don't try to help me,' they said. Now who was that? I wonder, I wonder . . .''

The major scowled. "You know, Ro . . . you're really starting to get on my nerves."

At that moment the door to the cabin swung open and an older Bajoran man came out. The wrinkles in his nose were fairly deep, and his hair was tinged with gray. He was cradling a fairly nasty-looking phaser weapon in his hand.

Without hesitation, he leveled the phaser at Ro, who made a point of raising her hands in the air. "What's going on out here?" he demanded.

From below, Kira called, "Cam! Is that you?!"

He looked down into the trap with a slightly puzzled air, as if he'd forgotten he set it. "Who is that?"

"It's me, Nerys! Kira Nerys!"

"Nerys?" He frowned in confusion at first, but then his face cleared. "Nerys! I'll be damned!"

Kira nodded. "You will if I have anything to say about it. Now get me out of this . . . this welcome mat you've set out!"

"Excuse me . . . can I lower my hands now?" Ro asked.

Comvic Cam looked at Ro and waved his phaser slightly, indicating the pit and acting as if he were reporting something that was news to her. "That's Kira Nerys!"

"Yes, I know. She decided to drop in."

Kira moaned rather loudly.

CHAPTER 6

CAM'S CABIN WAS not particularly spacious, but it was well-equipped. There were weapons, containers of food, water . . .

"Enough to last until forever and a half," Cam said proudly, as Kira and Ro sat down across from him in the small room. "I knew this would happen eventually. This disease, or something like it. I was prepared. I am completely secure. And there's more hidden away in other underground shelters I've built nearby."

"Where did you get it all?" Kira asked, looking around in wonderment. "I mean, this is amazing."

"Contacts," Cam said with smug confidence. "Although perhaps I shouldn't be telling you, Nerys. You are a government official now, working hand-in-hand with Starfleet. They might not appreciate some of the lengths I've gone to in order to reach my current status."

"Actually," Kira told him, "I don't think you're going to get all that much of a squawk over it. This isn't a Starfleet investigation, and we're not out to nail you, Cam. Actually, we need your help. We're trying to figure out where this awful disease came from."

"Haven't you heard?" Cam told her, sounding portentous. "It's the Wrath of the Prophets!"

Kira rolled her eyes. "Oh, please."

"No, really!" he insisted. "The Prophets sit there, clustered in their celestial temple, deep in the heart of the Bajoran wormhole, and they have judged us wanting. So we are being eliminated, Nerys. Wiped off the face of the planet. That is our destiny, our fate, for coming up lacking when the Prophets assessed our worth." Then he laughed coarsely. "At least, that's what's being bandied about."

"That's not it," Kira said flatly. "It's far more mundane than that. The tetrarch of the Paqu village decided to try her hand at the black market, and unfortunately had far less success than you. Bought a replicator and raw material that was contaminated. Now it's in the water supply, the food supply . . ."

"Not in mine," Cam said smugly.

Kira was disturbed by what sounded to her like a rather cavalier attitude, but she let it pass. After all, the man was an old comrade-in-arms.

"We're trying to retrace the lines of distribution," she explained, "to see where the replicator and the raw material originated."

Their host harrumphed. "It sounds like a waste of time."

"If it's just bad luck," Kira said, "then, yes, it might very well be a waste of time. But if this virus was deliberately planted, as some suspect . . . if it was a booby trap of some sort . . . then it's possible that whoever created it also knows the cure for it."

Cam nodded slowly, considering it. "Yesss . . . yes, it's possible."

"The tetrarch's direct purchasing contact was a Terran. He went by the name of Gnome."

The older man nodded. "Gnome, yes. If he's the one I'm thinking about, he changes his name as often as some of us change our socks."

"Perhaps more frequently than some of us," Ro put in. When Kira looked at her, Ro shrugged. "Sorry. I was feeling left out of the conversation."

As if Ro hadn't spoken, Kira continued. "It would seem he's changed his name again, because he's vanished. I don't know if he's off-planet, or if he's around but ducked into some hidey hole, or . . ."

"Dead?" Cam offered.

"Dead," she agreed. "That's also a possibility. And we've tried to track down his contacts as well, but we've had zero luck. Cam . . ." She leaned forward, fingers interlaced. "We need help. We need *your* help. Someone to point us in the right direction."

"I see." He paused, appearing to stare off into space.

Ro gave Kira a puzzled look, but Kira ignored it.

She wasn't concerned. Cam was obviously running through the possibilities in his head before—

"One hundred," he said at last.

Kira blinked in confusion. "One hundred. Is that . . . an address?"

As if he were surprised that he had to spell it out, Cam said, "One hundred bars of gold-pressed latinum."

The major regarded him. "What do you mean?"

"He means," Ro said, her voice flat and unamused, "that's how much he wants in payment for the information."

Kira looked from Ro to Cam and back again. She tried to force a smile, tried to find the joke.

"No," she said, "that can't be." She turned to her friend. "Cam, tell her that's not what you meant."

"You're asking me to finger people with whom I do business," Comvic said patiently. "I know you said Starfleet wasn't going to be sticking its nose in, and that this is purely a humanitarian effort. Nevertheless, you're something of a different animal these days, aren't you, Nerys? I don't know what to believe and what not."

"You can believe that people are dying!" she told him.

"People have been dying since people first existed, Nerys, and will continue to do so despite our best efforts. That's not my concern. My concern is that you're asking me to put myself out with no consideration for my welfare."

She stared at him disbelievingly. "By the Prophets,

you sound like a Ferengi," she said, making no attempt to hide the shock in her voice.

"Now, now," Comvic said, "we don't have to get insulting. Nerys, open your eyes. Look around this cabin. Look at the stock I've built up, everything I own. It may not look like much, but I have considerable holdings here and throughout Bajor.

"I've been aggressive the last couple of years. Done what I had to do to build up my personal fortune. I've managed an assortment of deals for others, made a few on my own behalf. A good deal of government contracting has been kicked my way, since I generally have a good feel as to who is . . . shall we say 'accessible?' I've handled bartering of land . . . mineral rights . . . food subsidies . . . anything you could name."

Kira started to speak, but Ro—rising immediately to the challenge—said coolly, "Children."

Kira Nerys turned to her old friend and waited for him to scoff at the notion. He didn't.

"Whatever's necessary," he said.

Kira clutched at her stomach, feeling ill. Cam saw her expression and requested, "Not on the carpet, please."

"People are dying!" she spat.

"We've been over that," he reminded her.

"No, we haven't," she told him. "By the Prophets, Cam, you risked your life when we fought together in the Shakaar! Risked it for no other reason than that it was the right thing to do!"

"I did it because it was the *only* thing to do. Having the Cardassians on our world was intolerable."

"Exactly!" Kira said. "Yes!"

"And now," he went on, "I do this—because it is likewise the only thing to do."

Kira felt her face flushing with anger. "No, Cam. You do this because you've changed into some sort of unrecognizable, selfish bastard. That's why you do this."

He shook his head sadly. "You always were naive, Nerys. Once upon a time, that was endearing. Now it's just tedious."

"Maybe I was naive," the major countered, making no attempt to hold back the waves of fury that washed over her. "Maybe I expected too much. I thought I could look to someone I admired to do the right thing, not out of self-aggrandizement, not out of self-enrichment, but simply because it was right."

He stared at her blandly for a moment, and then Kira pulled off the ornamental earring she wore. She tossed it on the small table in front of him.

"Here. What'll that get me? A name? A town? A fragment of a lead? Something so that we can save a few lives? Who knows, maybe we'll even save a child or two, so you can make a profit on them further down the line."

Comvic blanched. "Nerys, that was utterly unnecessary."

"No," she told him. "That was sarcasm. *This* is unnecessary."

And before she even had time to think about what she was doing, she slapped him hard across the face. The sound ricocheted through the cabin.

For a long moment, no one moved, and Comvic Cam didn't so much as raise a hand to rub his inflamed cheek. He simply sat there and stared at her.

Ro Laren slapped her thighs and got up. "Well," she said, "this has been enchanting. Truly. We'll be going now."

She pulled on Kira's arm. The major shook her off angrily.

"You make me sick," she told Comvic Cam.

His eyes expressionless, Comvic Cam replied, "There's a lot of that going around these days."

Kira spun on her heels and headed for the door, Ro directly behind her. They left the cabin, walking carefully around the booby trap that Comvic Cam had set for unsuspecting and unwanted visitors. Fury radiated from Kira like something palpable.

"Major," Ro began.

Kira rounded on her. "Don't say anything, Ro. Not a word. If you have to make some sort of noise, go back to whistl—"

"Oh, Nerys!"

The voice had come from behind them. They turned to see Comvic Cam standing in the doorway. He was holding Kira's ear ornament in his palm.

"Go to Ducoa," he said, "about ten miles west of here. Check around for a fellow named Sejup. He won't be hard to find; he's on the town council. You'd be amazed how many people I chat with are on town councils.

"Tell him I sent you. He doesn't deal in anything personally, but he knows people who know people. It's not the best information I could give you, but," he shrugged, "you get what you pay for."

Then, with a quick motion of his arm, he tossed the ornament to her.

She snatched it out of the air with one hand and stared at it. She started to say, "Cam, thank you."

But he had already closed the door.

"Lieutenant?"

Dax heard the word as if from a great distance.

"Lieutenant Dax?"

Abruptly, she remembered where she was and saw Mr. Hagen standing beside her. Turning to him, she did her best to appear efficient, on top of things.

"Yes, Mr. Hagen?"

The man frowned. "First Minister Shakaar is waiting to speak with you, sir. And I don't think he's too happy about it."

Glancing at her console, she saw the graphic that indicated a message from the Bajoran provisional government. How long had it been there? she wondered. How long had she been daydreaming?

"Thank you," she told Hagen. Then she put the first minister on her monitor.

Shakaar, a veteran freedom fighter with a mane of straw-colored hair, had probably been through more harrowing experiences than the Trill could count. Yet even he showed signs of the strain afflicting all Bajorans these days.

"Lieutenant Dax," he said, curbing his emotions as best he could, "there are a great many things demanding my attention lately, so I would appreciate it if you responded to my calls without delay."

Dax nodded, trying unsuccessfully to conceal her embarrassment. She couldn't seem to find a focus for herself. These daydreams—or whatever they were—kept drawing her somewhere else.

"My apologies, First Minister. What can I do for you?"

"I need good news," he told her. "And I'm certainly not going to find it down here. As if the illness itself wasn't bad enough, I've got the beginnings of a religious uprising on my hands."

The Lieutenant felt her jaw tighten. "What do you mean?"

Shakaar frowned. "My people have been through so much—and just when we were starting to make progress rebuilding our world, this happens. They fear the Prophets have grown angry with them—perhaps because it's taken them so long to rebuild Bajor. They believe the Prophets are the source of their virus. In fact, they're calling it the Wrath of the Prophets."

Dax shook her head. As close as she had become with Kira, she had never quite understood the depths of Bajoran spirituality. What they called the Prophets, for instance, were a group of sentient beings who resided in the spatial distortion known as the wormhole.

On the other hand, the faith of the Bajorans was what made them unique—what gave them their strength. And if ever they needed a source of strength, it was now.

"It's a plague," she agreed. "But no one's wrath, First Minister."

Shakaar grunted. "You and I know that, Lieutenant. But Kai Winn and some of the Vedeks are spewing nonsense to the contrary. No surprise, perhaps, since they're panicking themselves." He sighed softly. "But I didn't call to complain to you. I was hoping you'd made some progress analyzing the virus."

The Trill wished she could brighten his day. She said so. "Unfortunately, things are moving slowly—on all fronts. I know it's no consolation that we're working as hard as we can—"

The first minister held up his hand. "Don't think we don't appreciate what you're doing for us, Lieutenant. We *do*. I'll leave you alone to do your work. Shakaar out."

A moment later, the screen went dark. Dax stared at it. Maybe for a long time, maybe not. She couldn't tell.

All she knew was that when she looked up, she saw O'Brien standing next to her. Unlike Hagen, he didn't have any announcements to make. Only a cup of something hot and steaming in each hand.

The chief smiled sympathetically at her. "I thought

you might like something to drink," he said, and offered her one of the cups.

The Trill accepted it and took a sip. It was familiar to her somehow, but she couldn't place it.

"Thanks," she told him. "What is it?"

"Ginseng tea," he replied. "Keiko programmed it into the replicator. She claims it has remarkable healing powers, but, personally, I haven't seen any evidence of it." He smiled at her sheepishly. "And to be honest, I can't stand the taste. That's why I've got coffee in mine."

Dax took another sip. "Well," she said, "I kind of like it. Thanks." She glanced at the work crew on the far side of Ops. "How are they doing?"

O'Brien snorted. "Could be better. We fixed the ventilation problem, but we're getting those damned spikes here and there. As soon as we take care of them in one place, they pop up again someplace else. I have three teams scouring the station, rebuilding conduits and junction boxes as if they were going out of style."

Dax gazed into the amber-colored liquid in her cup. "I'm sure you'd have finished by now if you weren't covering for me all the time." She looked up at him. "I just don't know what's got me so distracted. I mean, of course I'm concerned about the plague and all—but I'm starting to think there's more to it. I just can't figure out what."

The chief didn't say anything. What *could* he say?

I can see you're perfectly useless, Jadzia, but don't worry about it. After all, I've got no worries of my own.

Just a wife and a daughter in the midst of a planet-wide plague.

"Listen," O'Brien told her at last, "why don't you take a break? You've been at this for a long time."

"So have you," Dax reminded him.

"Tell you what," he suggested. "Go unwind a bit. I'll take over in the meantime. And when you come back, it'll be my turn. To unwind, I mean."

The Trill regarded him. Why not? she asked herself. She wasn't much good to anybody up here anyway.

"All right," she agreed. "I'll be back in an hour."

The chief nodded approvingly.

But as Dax left, she couldn't avoid the feeling that she was abandoning her post. She felt she should be bent over her console, searching for something.

She just didn't know *what.*

Darkness was already settling in, so Kira and Ro had made a rough camp for the night. Kira lay on her back, looking up at the five moons of Bajor.

"Maybe you were right," she said at last.

"Of course I was." Ro was sitting up, keeping a wary eye on the fire that they had built for warmth. "Right about what?"

"What you said before. About Bajor being sick to its soul. About our people deserving to have this . . . this illness inflicted on them."

"I don't think I said 'deserved' exactly."

"Yes, that is precisely what you said, precisely the word you used. 'Deserved.' And then I said—"

"All right, all right, I don't need a word-for-word playback." The Maquis paused. "And now you think I was right about that."

"Comvic Cam was one of the best men I ever knew. To me, he was emblematic of everything right with Bajor."

Ro nodded. "I see. So now he can't help but be emblematic of everything wrong with Bajor. All the greed, the self-centeredness, symbolized in one tidy package. And faced with that, you start to wonder if perhaps the whole planet isn't worth the effort." She was quiet for a moment. "And what about the children, Major? I believe you brought that up. What about the innocent children?"

Kira sighed. "It always comes back to that, doesn't it, when you have any discussion like this. Do they deserve to suffer for the bankrupt soul of their elders?"

"I suppose it could be argued," Ro said, "that if they were allowed to grow to adulthood, they too would be infected by the moral and religious rot that's afflicted our people. That this is a sort of . . ."

"Mercy killing?" the major suggested.

Ro nodded.

Kira turned to look at her companion, and for the first time there was no hint of anything on her face other than naked pain. "What kind of deity would consider slaughtering innocents because of what they might become in the future? The only way that makes sense is if their cynicism and contempt for our way of life is a certainty. In which case, what happens to free will? What—"

"Major," Ro said softly, "can I point out something here? No matter what titles or job descriptions we presently have . . . no matter how we may want to define ourselves with our current goals . . . the bottom line is this: I'm a soldier. You're a soldier. Neither of us is the Kai, or a theologian.

"Hell," the Maquis went on, "I'm not even sure if I believe in the Prophets in the first place, and I know I don't believe they're skulking around in the Bajoran wormhole. Maybe, just maybe, we're out of our depth bandying this stuff around. But may I remind you that Comvic Cam, whom you seem to hold in such high regard, wound up helping us? Maybe he did it for a higher purpose. Maybe there's a glimmer of hope for us after all."

"Or maybe he just had a guilty conscience," Kira argued, "because of our past relationship."

"It's possible," Ro conceded. "It comes down, I suppose, to how positive a face you want to put on it."

Kira considered that for a moment and then said, "You want to know something?"

The Maquis grunted. "You'll probably tell me in any event, so I might as well say yes."

"When Cam was refusing to help us, I think the greatest part of my anger came from the embarrassment of knowing that you were sitting there, watching me look like an idiot."

Ro laughed softly. Kira was surprised to make note

of the fact that the woman had a surprisingly gentle laugh.

"Kira . . . looking like an idiot is one thing, but being an idiot is something else." Then she lay down and rolled over.

The major blinked. "I'm not sure if I'm supposed to take that as a compliment or not."

Ro yawned. "At this time of night, that's the best you're going to get out of me."

CHAPTER
7

VARIS SUL WAS looking at the same silvery moons Kira and Ro were sleeping under. But for Varis, there was no sleep.

Standing in her bedroom, in her nightclothes, there was only gnawing guilt and aggravation. And a hideous memory, sharper and more galling because of how recent it was. A memory of a great weight upon her, and a low chuckle that filled her soul with revulsion. . . .

And there was a sharp voice that barked behind her with unexpected ferocity.

"Are you out of your mind?" demanded Kai Winn.

Varis turned to regard the Kai, who stood across the room from her in her elegant white robes. The girl had always felt completely intimidated in dealing with

Winn, even when the Kai was "just" one of the 112 Vedeks who served as the spiritual counsel for Bajor.

That morning, Winn had come to the Paqu village to provide some sort of spiritual comfort for the ill, and for their caretakers. She had pulled the Paqu into prayer meetings, exhorting them to triumph over this hardship that had been thrown into their lives.

The Paqu had listened attentively, mesmerized by the Kai's unmistakable personal strength and charisma. There had been only one unfortunate hitch during the Kai's discourse, and that was when a villager had keeled over, stricken by the illness, and had to be carried away to his home.

The disease had picked up a name—"Wrath of the Prophets." Varis counted herself lucky. It could just as easily have been named after her.

"Well?" Kai Winn was demanding. "I ask again, child, are you out of your mind?"

Varis stared at her. Once upon a time, she would have been grateful for the loose nightclothes she was wearing. They would have served to hide the trembling of her legs.

Now, however, she felt oddly detached from the situation. The threat of the Kai's anger was a distant second to what she had been through in the past night and day.

His breath had been foul, and he had said things . . .

Once again she tried to shake off the memory as she said, "You speak of the cure, I assume."

Kai Winn approached her. Her voice was trembling, but it wasn't with fear.

"It's true, then? Your dabbling in black market and illicit goods hasn't brought sufficient disaster? You have actually made inquiries about returning to that same ghastly source?"

Varis nodded. "To see if a cure could be found, yes. I put out some feelers, spoke with some people . . ."

"Have you learned nothing?" the Kai demanded.

"What I've learned," Varis said calmly, "is that when one makes a mistake, one should try to rectify it . . ."

Winn glared at her. "By repeating that mistake? Then you've learned nothing."

Silently, Varis walked across the room and slid open the drawer of a cabinet. She pulled out a small vial from within and held it up.

"What is that?" Kai Winn demanded.

"A possible antidote."

Winn's mouth moved for a moment, but no sound came out. "Antidote?" she asked at last.

Varis watched the Kai's reaction and drew a measure of strength from it. "Yes. Obtained through black-market sources. Not the same individual from whom I got the replicator in the first place; he's disappeared, and in any event, we parted on . . . not the best of terms. So I made connections with a trader named Tabatch. He came to the village last night, snuck in to meet with me, and provided me with this."

Winn held out her hands. "Give it to me, child."

"What?" Varis said. She felt her confidence building with every moment. "Aren't you going to lecture me? Tell me how wrong I was? Scold me within an inch of my life? Berate me and . . ."

"We don't have time for this nonsense!" the Kai cried. "I am telling you to give it to me!"

Varis tossed the vial to her. She threw it with a sweeping underhanded gesture, and it fell a foot short of Winn's outstretched fingers. The vial hit the floor . . .

. . . and shattered.

A thick blue liquid spread out, soaking the wood floor, and the Kai let out a shriek of despair. "You . . . I . . . !"

"It's no good," Varis told her.

Winn looked at her in confusion. "What do you mean?"

The tetrarch sighed. "Do you seriously think I had something like this in my possession for this long and did nothing with it? I've already had it examined and tested."

"And . . . ?"

"And it was worthless. The price I paid for it was wasted. It does nothing to slow the progress of the plague."

"Hunh." Winn digested this information and said, "I knew it. This is what happens when you trade in—"

"You knew it?" Varis Sul said skeptically. "Oh, please . . ."

"I will thank you to watch how you address me!" the Kai ordered.

"And I will thank you not to treat me like a fool," said the young woman. "I saw your expression, your excitement, when I said I had a possible antidote. You didn't care that it had come through the black market. You didn't care about anything except achieving the goal."

Her voice rose with anger. "Earthers talk of the ends justifying the means, and that's what I did when I was trying to save my people from starving. And that's what you've done in your own career, Kai."

Winn tried to interrupt in her customary high-handed tone. But Varis would have none of it, steamrolling right over her elder's protests.

"You think I don't know? You think everyone doesn't know? By the Prophets, you're blind! We all know of your machinations and your plans and schemes, so don't you dare stand there in judgment of me—because when it comes to self-serving and single-mindedness, I can't even begin to operate on your level!"

The Kai was trembling with anger. "You think you can talk to me in that manner?"

"I don't think it," Varis said flatly. "I've already done it." She gathered herself. "I tried to help. I did what I thought was best for the community. And because of that—because of those good intentions—people are dying. And here's the ironic part, in case you haven't noticed."

She tapped her chest. "I haven't contracted it. Oh, I'm sure I will, at some point. My blood has already been drawn and checked, and there's no particular immunity factors in it. It's just the luck of the draw. Or . . . here's an even more interesting thought . . . it's the will of the Prophets. For my having committed the unpardonable sin of trying to save lives, they're going to make certain that I live as long as possible, so that I can see my whole village come down with the Wrath."

Varis swallowed. "You know what that says to me? It says that if the Prophets are looking down on us, pronouncing judgment on us, then they are a petty and pathetic bunch of bastards. They find us wanting? Well, I pronounce judgment on them—and I tell them to go to hell."

The Kai looked down and said nothing at first. Finally she replied.

"I shall pray for you, my child. I shall pray that guidance is given to your soul to bring it back to salvation. The Prophets test us, and how we respond to those tests is a measure of . . ."

Varis grunted. "Save it, Kai Winn. Save the platitudes for your next sermon. Save the dogma for someone who cares. I'm already damned. I've known that since this entire sorry mess first started. If the Prophets are doing this to test our faith, well . . . they've already got their answer from this quarter."

The Kai drew herself up and said, "I will pray for you . . . nonetheless."

Varis shrugged. "Go ahead, for all the good it will do any of us."

* * *

Sisko gazed at the jumbled gray amalgam that hung in space in front of him. It was constructed of various ship fragments and antiquated station parts and a few components he'd never seen before in his life.

"Mephil Trantos." Quark chuckled.

The human grunted. "Doesn't look like much to me," he said.

The Ferengi shrugged. "That's because you haven't spent some of your fondest moments in this place. There's no manner of vice that can't be fulfilled here, no itch that can't be scratched—and by professionals. I remember these two absolutely luscious Pandrilites . . ."

"I don't want to hear about it," Sisko told him.

"Twin sisters." Quark sighed, continuing his ruminations undeterred. "Arrenya and Tensata. Tall, muscular . . . quite lovely." His hand rose instinctively to one of his earlobes. "Had their own stage show. And the things those ladies could do with a venn'ga frond—"

Sisko leaned closer. "I *said* I don't want to *hear* it, Quark."

The Ferengi sighed again, then cast a look of disapproval at his companion. "You know the trouble with you, Captain? You don't get out enough. Not nearly."

"Whatever you say," Sisko told him. "Now, you're certain we won't have any problem disembarking here?"

"None," Quark assured him. "The Orions don't make money by turning people away."

"Even Starfleet officers?" the human asked.

"They'd welcome a Klingon targ if they thought he'd brought some latinum," the Ferengi replied. "Relax, Captain." He leaned back in his seat. "I know *I* will."

Sisko frowned. "Quark, I didn't bring you here for a vacation. You said you'd introduce me to the Orion trade administrator."

"I said I'd *take* you to him," the Ferengi reminded him. "There's a difference, you know."

Sensing a scam, the human rounded on him. "Quark . . ."

The Ferengi held up his hand in a plea for peace. "I haven't forgotten our objective here, I assure you. It's just that we'll do better if we split up. That way, you can try your approach . . . and I can try mine."

Sisko had to admit there was a certain utility to the plan. "So I'll . . . work on the trade administrator by myself?"

"That's a good idea," Quark replied. "And I'll work the gaming den." He smiled, so that the points of his teeth showed. "Who knows? I might get lucky."

The human didn't say anything this time. He just cast a withering look at his companion.

The Ferengi assumed his most innocent demeanor. "I *meant* in getting hold of some answers," he explained. "Really, Captain. You've got to learn to trust me a little more."

Sisko turned to his instruments and began to hail

the station. "I'd sooner trust that targ you were talking about."

Jake Sisko lay draped over the couch in his quarters, unable to get the image of the dying Bajorans out of his head. Here he was, safe and sound, while far below him on the planet's surface, people were losing their lives. It was remarkable to him that they had all these facilities aboard *Deep Space Nine*—medical, defensive, offensive, what have you—and yet they were helpless to aid people in need.

There was a beeping over his communications screen. Jake rolled off the couch, walked over, and answered it. To his surprise, Varis Sul's image appeared on the screen.

"Sul!" he said. "You're . . . you're all right!"

She smiled gamely. "About as all right as one could be, given the circumstances. Is your father there, Jake? I know this is after hours, so I was hoping to catch him in . . ."

"He's gone," Jake said. "Trying to help find the source of the bad replicator material." He frowned. "Are you really okay?"

"Jake." She sighed. "I'd be lying if I said things were going well."

He nodded sympathetically. "What did you want to talk to my father about?"

"I just . . . wanted an update," Varis said. "I know your people are working in tandem with our . . . *government.*" She paused over the word, her disdain for that august body clear in her tone. "Working to deal with this affliction. I wanted to know how it was going. And I wanted . . ." Her voice trailed off.

Jake sat down in the chair by the monitor. "Wanted what?" he asked.

"Hope, I suppose. Something to cling to."

He shrugged. "It'll be okay, Sul. With everybody working so hard to fight this thing, it doesn't stand a chance."

She looked at him more intently. "And tell me, Jake . . . if the news were dismal, the situation hopeless . . . would you be able to tell me that? Would you have the resolve to look into my eyes and say, 'Sul, my old friend . . . there's every likelihood that you're going to die before help can reach you.' Could you tell me that, Jake?"

The captain's son shifted uncomfortably in his chair. "I . . . sure. Sure, I could be honest with you like that." Except he couldn't have been, and he knew it . . . and from the look on his face, Varis had to know it, too.

"You're a very sweet young man, Jake," Varis said slowly, "and I wish that things could have gone differently."

He became angry with her, just for a moment. "Stop talking like that, Sul. It's going to work out. We just have to wait, just have to be patient . . ."

"Yes," she said, "that's what I'm always told. Sit and wait." Her voice began to grow taut with outrage. "I waited for my government to sort matters out and feed my people, and it did no good. And so I took matters into my own hands, and now they're dying.

"But you know what, Jake? You know what? For a brief time, at least, my people were happy. It may not have turned out the way I wanted, but at least for one moment, there was hope.

"And if my choice is to sit around and be hopeless, or take some sort of action and fight for hope once more, then I would do the same thing again. And again."

Jake tried to deepen his voice a bit, to take on his father's characteristic air of infinite reasonability. "Sul . . . it's not entirely in your hands anymore. The Bajorans excel at having faith. That's what you have to have now—faith that we'll come through for you. Faith that a cure will be found."

"Faith." She sighed. "Believe me, nothing would serve me in better stead than to be able to cling to faith. Unfortunately . . . I don't think that's really possible anymore. And until it is, I don't really think I deserve to be tetrarch. I'm not even entirely sure I should be Bajoran."

"Sul," he said, "you're talking crazy."

"Goodbye, Jake."

"Now wait a—"

But the screen blinked off. Leaping to his feet, Jake tried to call her back. But she didn't reply. He thumped the padd below the screen in frustration.

"Ohhh, Sul, don't do anything stupid, please," he prayed.

Unfortunately, prayers weren't being answered in any sort of positive manner these days. Not around Bajor, anyway.

Varis Sul heard the beeping from the communications screen, but she didn't bother to answer it. She knew who it was from, and she knew what he wanted to say. But truthfully . . . there was no point in further communication. Everything that could be said already had been.

She was busy packing supplies. Supplies, her small phaser, and whatever other items were easily transportable and might be of use.

By morning, she would be gone. Gone to find a cure, a real cure this time. Gone to find vengeance for her people against the insidious scheme that had been launched in order to destroy them. A scheme so insidious that many of them didn't even realize that it had to be deliberate.

Out of habit, as Varis prepared to head out the door, she started to say a quick prayer to the Prophets, asking that they watch over her. Then she thought about recent events and decided that would be the last thing she was inclined to do. She'd be damned if she would give the Prophets that kind of satisfaction.

Then again, as she had so sullenly told Kai Winn . . . she was damned anyway.

CHAPTER
8

BENZAR OKRIN HAD laughed in Kira's face.

"Me?" he had said. "Kira . . . you've known me for years. How could you possibly think I'd have anything to do with any of this?"

And, indeed, she had known Benzar Okrin for years. He hadn't precisely been part of the liberation movements with which she had fought, but he had been known as a supplier of weaponry and safehouses when Kira or any of her people were in need.

Benzar had been extremely expert at working both sides of the fence, with the result that he had risen to a fairly respectable rank in his community. At the same time, he was counted on as a friend by those who wanted Bajor free of Cardassian influence.

Kira and Ro had sat across from him, on the

opposite side of his large and imposing desk. As a prelate in the community of Tindar, he had certain perks to which he was entitled. An impressive office and an excellent view were two of them.

"You know, Okrin, there was a time when I'd never have dreamed of suspecting you." Kira had sat with her legs crossed at the knees, her fingers interlaced. "But lately I've been chatting with a lot of people. Seen a variety of old friends. Been everywhere from Sorshaq to Ducoa to Mexal, and now here. It's been something of a twisty road, and now your name has entered into the mix."

"And people have been talking to you?" Benzar had smiled. He was fairly close in age to Kira, with wide-set eyes and a big open face.

She had shrugged. "Some willingly, some less so."

"Some, we had to beat it out of them," Ro had said flatly.

The major had eyed her friend Okrin. "I want to know if you've got any connections in the black market. Any dealings at all."

The prelate's smile had widened. "And if I don't tell you, you or your friend will beat it out of me?" Benzar had seemed most amused by the idea. Or he had been until Ro had reached across his very large desk, grabbed a fistful of his shirt, and yanked him back across it. His chin had thudded hard on the desktop and he had let out a yelp of anger.

"That's right," Ro snarled.

"Ro, let him go! Now!" Kira had said.

"I'm tired of pussyfooting around with your old friends, Major," Ro had snapped at her. "I'm tired of playing things your way. We're running out of time and Bajor is soon going to start running out of people. Now, this slug is going to tell us what we want to know, and he's going to tell us now!"

Kira had pulled Ro's hand free of Benzar's shirt. "We'll do this my way," she had insisted.

"Get out!" Benzar had bellowed, staggering to his feet. "Do you hear me? Get out! I have nothing to do with any of this, and you will get out of my office now!"

They had exited quickly, and Kira had turned to Ro. "Next time," she said, "warn me when you're planning to play a game of 'good cop, bad cop.'"

"Never heard of it," Ro had replied, and walked quickly down the hallway with Kira following.

That had been how the afternoon had gone. The evening was going somewhat differently.

Kira and Ro were sticking to the shadows as they watched Benzar Okrin make his way through the streets. Every so often he would stop and look over his shoulder, clearly trying to make sure that he wasn't being followed.

"I don't like this," Ro whispered. "It's too easy."

"Too easy?" Kira echoed. "What do you mean?"

"I mean," said the Maquis, "if he has some sort of meeting scheduled, why is he going there himself? Why doesn't he send an envoy or messenger? Why risk himself?"

The major grunted. "Because Benzar has two significant character traits. First, he's overconfident. Second, he's a control freak. He likes to do everything himself rather than trust anyone, and he's eminently confident that he'll never get caught."

"Why is that?" Ro asked.

"Possibly because he's never been caught." Kira gestured for Ro to follow her, and kept close after Benzar . . . but not too close.

They tracked him across town and at one point nearly lost him. But then, after a few frantic minutes of doubling back, they found him again. . . .

And he was with someone.

From around a building corner, Kira squinted through the darkness. "Is that . . . what I think it is?"

Ro nodded in confirmation. "It's an Orion, all right. You really have to work on overcoming this perpetual state of shock you're in."

In a low and angry voice, Kira hissed at her. "Listen, maybe *you* never found anyone or anything to believe in. Maybe you never—"

She stopped herself, remembering where she was and what she was doing there. Then she went on, in a much more measured tone.

"Maybe you never found a cause that went so deeply into your soul you would have done anything to support it, even given your life for it. But I had a cause like that, and I had people who shared it with me. And now, one by one, I'm finding they're all knee-deep in some sort of graft or corruption."

"I see," said the Maquis. "And what's your point,

exactly? You're upset because you're thinking how easily it could have been you?"

"That," Kira said, stabbing a finger in the direction of Benzar and his Orion partner, "could never have been me."

Ro chuckled dryly. "You wouldn't be this upset if you really believed that. And you know what's really amazing, Major? With just a twist or two of fate—if things had sightly zigged instead of zagging—*I* could have been you."

Kira looked at her. "Ro Laren on *Deep Space Nine* instead of me. That's laughable."

"You don't hear *me* laughing."

They lapsed into silence then, Kira still burning over what she was seeing. The Orion seemed to hand something over to Benzar, and Benzar gave him something in return. Benzar slid it into his jacket pocket. Then the Orion melted into the shadows and Benzar began to retrace his steps, heading toward home.

He got three blocks before Kira and Ro yanked him into the shadows. The prelate started to cry out, unable to see his attackers, no doubt thinking he was being robbed—but Ro clamped a hand over his mouth. Then Kira shoved her hand into Benzar's pocket and withdrew a half-dozen small gleaming spheres.

"Well, well," she said. "Orion energy orbs. Nice little haul you've got for yourself here, Benzar. And what did you give him in return, huh?"

Benzar tore Ro's hand away from his mouth. "It's not what you think, Nerys!"

"Actually," said the major, "it's exactly what I think. And don't call me Nerys. Not ever again. I don't give you that privilege. You know . . . this time I'm drawing a line, Benzar. This time I don't care about whatever information you might have to offer. This time I'm just dragging you straight to the authorities."

"Yes, by all means, do that," Benzar told her, his startled voice gaining strength. "And how will you know who to bring me to, eh?"

Slowly his meaning became clear to her. Her voice low and angry, she said, "What are you telling me? That people above you are in on this?"

"You want us to believe that the entire Bajoran government is on the take?" Ro put in skeptically.

Benzar laughed nervously. "The entire government, no. But enough. In all probability, you'd turn me over to someone who's going to turn me loose almost immediately—after sharing a few drinks and laughing with me over your ineptitude. And just about everyone else in the provisional government, even those who aren't a part of it, know what's going on and don't want to get their hands dirty.

"They turn a blind eye to it. And why not? Until this mess in the Paqu village, just about everything that came into Bajor through the black market was beneficial. Who wants to stand in the way of something that serves the public good? So you see, Kira, the chances of you bringing me to anyone who's going to try and prosecute me . . . well, the odds are pretty slim."

In a hard tone, the major said, "I'll take that chance. Come on." And she started to drag him out of the alleyway.

"Okay, wait . . . wait," Benzar said suddenly. He shrugged in a surprisingly nonchalant fashion. "Who knows . . . you may be lucky. Certainly you have been enough in the past. All right, listen. You've been chasing all over, but there's really only one person who's going to have the answers you want. He's extremely well connected."

Kira eyed him. "Name."

"Manimoujak. He's an Yridian trader."

"Where can we find him?" Ro demanded.

Benzar didn't even acknowledge that she had spoken. Instead his full attention was on Kira.

"Remember that bunker you holed up in once? After the Gallitep camp was liberated and you needed somewhere to hide?"

She thought for a moment. "Of course. Outside of Sorshaq."

"Oh, wonderful," Ro muttered. "After all this, we're traveling in a circle."

"Well, that's where he is." Benzar hesitated, and then said, "I never had the chance to tell you, Kira, because we didn't have all that much face-to-face contact in those days . . . but I had a nephew who got out of that camp because of you. Threats aside, intimidation aside . . . I owe you for that, at least. Here." He pressed the orbs into Kira's hand.

"Is this supposed to be a bribe?" the major demanded.

"Yes," Benzar said, "but not for you. Manimoujak isn't going to be browbeaten, and he has no better nature to appeal to. This"—he gestured to the orbs—"is the only thing he'll understand."

"What will it buy us?" asked Kira.

"Information, if he has it. A cure if he can obtain it."

Ro shook her head in disbelief. "Charming. So we'll be dealing with a man who apparently is capable of saving a planetful of people . . . for the right price."

"Not everyone is motivated out of the goodness of their heart," Benzar said.

"Believe me, Okrin," Kira said ruefully, "I've figured that out."

The prelate nodded and then started off down the street. After a second or two, Kira called after him.

"Okrin . . . thank you."

He smiled. "Don't mention it. To anyone."

The dining hall on Mephil Trantos was hot and smoky and noisy enough to wake the dead, and full of exotic scents Sisko had no great desire to identify. One of the strongest of them rose from an Orion firepot in the center of the heavy wooden table before him.

The firepot, made of some iron alloy, was an ancient and ornate piece of work embossed with crudely erotic scenes extracted from Orion mythology. The thing's hourglass-shaped lower cylinder was packed with hot coals, which provided the heat needed to cook the variety of wing slugs still swimming in the several bowls above. The bowls, in turn, rested on a charred metal framework.

As the human looked on, the corpulent green-skinned Orion who'd been identified to him as Kestralnamen—nominally this sector's trade administrator, but really nothing more than the head pirate—lifted one of the bowls in his heavily padded gauntlets and tilted his head back.

His dark bulging eyes danced with anticipation as he scrutinized his treat, reveling in the wing slugs' faint high-pitched screams. Then, before the sleek black creatures could quite boil to death, he poured the bowl's steaming, writhing contents into his mouth.

Fortunately for Sisko, he'd dined with Klingons on more than one occasion. After Rokeg bloodpie, Orion wing slugs didn't seem quite so bad.

Kestralnamen shook the bowl a couple of times to dislodge any choice tidbits that may have gotten stuck to its sides. Then, wiping his mouth with the back of one gauntlet, he replaced the bowl in its holder.

"Now, then," he asked the human, "what kind of information were you looking for?"

Sisko had an urge to tell the Orion a tiny piece of wing slug was clinging to his chin—or one of them, anyway. However, it seemed more important right now to get to the point.

"Information on trade between the Orions and the Bajorans," he replied. "Specifically with regard to a shipment of food replicators delivered to Bajor just a couple of weeks ago."

Kestralnamen belched—an action as surprising to him, apparently, as it was to the human. It required all of Sisko's willpower not to turn his face from the resultant stench.

"We did not supply these replicators," the Orion pointed out. "In fact, we do not trade with Bajor at all. Our last transaction with the Bajorans was before their occupation by the Cardassians."

Kestralnamen leaned forward to consider the other three bowls in the firepot. They had been placed over the coals on a staggered schedule so they wouldn't all reach their peaks at once.

It appeared to Sisko the contents of the bowl on the Orion's near left was almost ready for consumption. Judging from the way Kestralnamen was licking his lips, he thought so, too.

The human smiled. "You don't trade with the Bajorans officially, perhaps. In other words, not with the provisional government. But we both know that transactions take place from time to time."

The Orion removed another bowl from the firepot. "Do we?" he asked.

"Don't we?" Sisko rejoined, playing the game.

Kestralnamen shrugged. "As far as I can tell, no Orion has even made an overture to do business with the Bajorans. And as administrator of this sector, I would be privy to any and all transactions."

Sisko knew the Orion wasn't telling him the truth. He also knew it would be highly impolitic to say so.

Then again, he wasn't getting anywhere by being polite. "You," he told Kestralnamen, "are lying through your teeth."

The administrator's eyes slitted. He glanced at the human. "I would say this audience is over," he remarked. Then he emptied the second bowl into his mouth.

Sisko frowned. Apparently, he'd come a long way for a very short conversation. He had only one trump card left, and he played it.

"You know," he said, "it's too bad."

Wiping his mouth with the back of his gauntlet again, Kestralnamen grunted. "What's too bad?"

The human stood up, came around the side of the table, and leaned close to the Orion's ear. "What if I were to tell you I could prepare a bowl of wing slugs that would make your head spin?"

Kestralnamen looked at him suspiciously. "And how would you do that?"

Sisko smiled. "My dad is a chef in New Orleans, back on Earth. He taught me all he knew—and he had a hot sauce men would kill for."

The Orion swallowed with anticipation. "A hot sauce?"

The human nodded. "That's right. Of course, I don't give out the recipe to just anyone. Only to my friends." He leaned even closer. "My friends tell me what I want to know, Administrator. Are you one of my friends?"

For a long promising moment, Sisko thought he'd struck paydirt. Then a scowl spread over Kestralnamen's fat ugly face.

"You try my patience," he snapped. "I told you all there is to tell. Now leave me to my meal, damn you, or I'll—"

He was interrupted by a commotion from across the room. Someone had opened the door to the gaming room. And the one cry the captain heard over all the others was: "Dabo!"

What's more, he recognized the voice. It was Quark's. Apparently the Ferengi was playing dabo instead of digging for information.

I might have known, Sisko mused.

He turned back to Kestralnamen. "Perhaps you're right," he said. "This isn't the best time to discuss the matter. We can renew our discussion after you've eaten."

The Orion frowned. "There's nothing more to discuss," he insisted, and left before the captain could argue otherwise.

Sisko glanced at the open door to the gaming room. Kestralnamen was clearly a dead end—at least for the time being. That meant Quark's role in this mission was looming larger and larger.

And he wasn't going to get them what they'd come for by playing dabo. Pulling down on the front of his tunic, the captain crossed the dining hall and headed for the gaming room.

He had a few choice words for his erstwhile partner—and none of them were "dabo."

It took a while for him to make his way through the crowd. It seemed Quark was on a hot streak, and the onlookers were packed as tight as Solemian sardines. Finally Sisko reached the first rank, just behind the Ferengi.

Quark was on the verge of spinning the wheel again. It was only the captain's voice in his ear that made him hesitate.

"This is *not* why we came here," Sisko grated.

The Ferengi smiled at the other players around the dabo table. Out of the corner of his mouth, he said, "I'm trying to build a little trust, if you don't mind. Now move along before you wreck everything."

The captain glared at him. As far as he could tell, all Quark was building was a pile of chips—and a healthy one at that.

Still, the Ferengi had his own ways of doing things—ways that had apparently worked well for him in the past. And Sisko *had* promised to extend a little trust.

For the time being, the captain retreated through the crowd and returned to the dining hall next door. He decided he would give Quark all the latitude he needed—at least for now.

Mount Kataba was a tough climb. As they approached the foot of it, Kira could see that Ro was beginning to appreciate that fact.

The Maquis tilted her head back, eyes fixed on the lofty tree-covered crag. "You have got to be kidding," she said.

"It wouldn't be much of a hidden bunker if it were sitting out in plain sight, now, would it?" Kira demanded.

Ro looked at her askance. "It's a mountain. It's a damned mountain."

"I know the paths," the major assured her. "They're steep and treacherous, but they're also handy when you're trying to avoid pursuers." She folded her arms and studied Ro with an unmistakable air of superiority. "What's the matter, Ro? Feel you're not up to it?"

The Maquis chuckled humorlessly. "I can climb anything you toss at me. I just hope I'm not wasting my time."

"You signed on with me," Kira reminded her, "so your time is mine to waste."

"You know," Ro said slowly, "I am getting pretty damned sick of you."

"Oh, are you?"

"Yes, I am." The Maquis unslung her backpack and tossed it to the ground. "I'm getting sick of your constant whining over how nothing and nobody from your checkered past is as good as you remember. I'm sick of your overbearing overconfidence. I'm sick of the way you look at me . . ."

Kira tilted her head. "And how do I look at you, precisely?"

"Like I'm not good enough to be working with you. Like I'm some . . ."

"Some disgraced deserter?"

Ro's features hardened. "You act as if you have an exclusive right to moral outrage. You shove me into the background and try to run a show that hasn't been running particularly well."

"You think you can do better?" Kira asked.

"I think you should stop thinking you're better than me just because you landed on *Deep Space Nine* . . . and I landed in a Starfleet stockade."

"That's not the reason I think I'm better than you."

Ro smiled in triumph. "So you admit it."

"Yes, I admit it," Kira said defiantly. "It's because when I take on a job, and I take an oath, and I take responsibilities, I stick to them. I don't find excuses or look for greener pastures. I do the job."

"Even when you realize the job has gone sour?"

Kira shook her head. "Your job never went sour, Ro. You did."

The Maquis glared at her for a long moment, then started to walk away. Kira called after her. "Quitting again?"

Ro whirled, looking daggers at Kira, and stooped to reach for her backpack. "I was just going to pick up my pack. Do you mind?"

"Thank you for clarifying that," Kira said.

"You're welcome. So let's get to this blasted bunker already."

Once more, the major led the way. And this time, it was Ro who gave the silent treatment to Kira. The silence suited Kira just fine.

She moved quickly up the mountain path, surefootedly finding just the right nooks and crevices to give her the occasional finger or toe hold she needed.

Kira had forgotten how clean the air was up here,

how breathtaking the view. To the east, a blanket of overgrown farmland stretched to the horizon, basking in unbroken sunlight. To the west, she could see even bigger peaks than Kataba, shouldering a pile of fleecy clouds.

But this was no time for sightseeing, she reminded herself. This was business.

The path wound its way higher and higher. At one point, it branched off. Kira slowed, looking around in momentary uncertainty.

From behind, Ro said with ill-concealed derision, "What's the matter, pathfinder? Feeling a little lost?"

"You'll pardon me if, unlike certain people, I give some thought to where I'm going. It's been sixteen years, after all. Wait."

Kira moved to the right, feeling small standing there with mountains rising on either side of her. She pushed aside some brush, revealing a small mark, a half circle that wouldn't have meant anything to anyone else.

"I thought so. This way."

Ro looked concerned. "How do you know?"

"Because sixteen years ago, I carved this marker into the rock so I'd always know which way to go. As I said . . . some people actually plan their lives."

"And some people become overly regimented and dull," her companion retorted.

They made it up and over a plateau. Kira pointed. "There. Over there."

"Over where?"

"Just past there. I know at least two hidden entrances to it. But you can't really see it until you're right on top of it."

They crossed the plateau. It was eerily silent to Kira. She had no reason to expect it to be noisy, of course, but somehow the silence felt oppressive. Even wrong, for some reason.

"I don't like this," Ro said. "Something stinks. Let's get out of here."

Kira looked at her contemptuously. "'Let's get out of here'? Spoken like a true deserter."

"I'm telling you, this is—"

Ro was interrupted by the unmistakable *klak* of energy-bolt cartridges being slammed into Yridian blasters.

Kira estimated there were a half-dozen of them, aimed at her and Ro from different points in the mountainous terrain around them. Ten yards in front of them, there was a whirring of gears and motors, and the ground seemed to rise up. The main entranceway to the bunker, a large gleaming metal cylinder, was now plainly in evidence.

An Yridian slowly emerged from the main entrance. He was hideously wrinkled, even for someone of his race.

"You are Manimoujak?" Kira asked.

He nodded. "And you are Kira." He looked to her companion. "And Ro. You have half-a-dozen power orbs that belong to me."

"To you?" the major asked. Ro sighed and rolled her eyes.

"Yes," the Yridian explained. "Benzar Okrin told

me you would be delivering them . . . and yourselves . . . in due time."

"Delivering ourselves," Kira said. "Nooo . . . I
don't think so. We're not part of any bargain."

"Oh yes you are," Manimoujak insisted. And that
was the last thing Kira heard before something hard
slammed into her head, sending her spiraling into
unconsciousness.

Manimoujak stared down at the insensate forms of
the two females. He stroked his chin.

"I wonder how much they'll go for on the Orion
trade market," he said out loud.

One of his lieutenants said, "Benzar warned they
could be pretty feisty."

"Good," Manimoujak said approvingly. "That's
the way Orions like their slaves—strong and spirited.
Drag them inside . . . but be sure not to damage
them. We wouldn't want them to be in anything other
than mint condition."

A moment later, his men complied.

CHAPTER
9

FOLLOWING O'BRIEN'S ADVICE that she unwind, Dax found herself sitting at a table in Quark's. Despite the proprietor's absence, the service was as quick as ever, and the Scandavian Sunsets just as good.

The lieutenant liked Quark's. It was a true melting pot of races from throughout the galaxy. When one had lived as many lives as she had, one was more than used to diversity—one reveled in it.

And, of course, Morn was sitting at the bar, an ongoing part of that diversity. Some things never changed, she mused. Bajor orbited its sun every day and Morn could always be found at Quark's.

As she sipped her drink, Dax watched Rom, Quark's brother, scurry past her with a large board.

Rom was not known for his initiative, but he was still a Ferengi. Ergo, he was up to something.

When an Andorian rose from his chair, Rom grabbed it and moved it closer to the entrance to the bar. Then he got up on the chair with his board and placed the thing above the door.

Stepping back on the chair, the Ferengi surveyed his handiwork. Apparently unsatisfied, he moved the board a little to his left. Next, he produced a small cloth from inside his waistcoat and polished a smudge on the board's lower right corner.

That done, Rom got down off the chair again, crossed to the bar, and grabbed a shimmering sheet that absorbed and reflected the light in golds and yellows. Returning to the board with the sheet under his arm, he hung it over the sign, studied its draping, and then beamed.

Passing Dax on his way toward the labyrinth of back rooms, Quark's brother was still smiling. Unable to see the front of the board and what it said, the Trill put her hand on the Ferengi's sleeve.

"Running a special?" she asked.

Rom looked at her. "Oh, no." He grinned and jerked a thumb over his shoulder in the direction of the board. "You know where my brother went . . ."

Dax nodded. "Of course."

"The Orions are a dangerous people," the Ferengi explained. "And they won't like Captain Sisko poking around. I was just being prepared."

She nodded in understanding. "I hope it won't come to that, Rom."

The Ferengi made a face. "Well, me, too," he said. "Quark is my brother, after all. But you know the Sixth Rule of Acquisition."

It took the Trill a moment to recall the specific rule—never easy with 285 of them to sift through—but given the circumstances, she was able to figure it out. "Never allow family to stand in the way of opportunity."

Rom snorted in nervous laughter and bobbed his head, grinning wider than before. "You see my point, then."

Dax grunted. "In a way, I suppose I do."

"Miss your brother?" came a gruff voice.

The Trill turned at the same time Rom did—to see Odo standing there. It was as if the constable had come out of nowhere, which—in Odo's case—was actually within the realm of possibility.

The Ferengi cringed a bit. Then he puffed up his chest and announced, "Welcome to Rom's Pleasure Palace. What may I serve you? On the house, of course."

"That's very generous of you," Odo said, "considering I don't drink—and we both know it." He tilted his head to indicate the entrance. "Interesting new name for the place."

Rom shuffled a bit. "Do you know our one hundred and Sixty-second Rule of Acquisition?" he asked.

Odo shook his head. "And what would that be?" he asked disdainfully.

Rom smiled. " 'Even in the worst of times, someone

turns a profit.' Now, I may not be a very good businessman, but I'm still a Ferengi."

The constable grunted. "So you are."

With nothing left to say, Rom hurried off, snapping out orders to waiters and bartenders—and sounding frighteningly like Quark. Silently wishing the hard-luck Ferengi good fortune, the Trill sipped at her drink again.

Odo turned to her. "Any luck?" he asked.

Dax shook her head. "Not yet."

The shapeshifter didn't comment any further. Maybe he knew how many people had inquired about the doctor's progress in the last several hours. Or maybe he just sensed when to go easy. In any case, Dax found herself grateful for the respite.

Suddenly a bizarre and unfamiliar sound intruded on them—a sound that reminded the Trill too much of someone choking. Rising, she took a quick look around the place—and saw Morn slumping against the bar, his wrinkled dark skin starting to turn pale, tears streaming down his long face. His right hand trembled a bit, just enough to slosh liquid over the edge of his glass.

He wasn't in danger of choking, as she first thought. But there was definitely something wrong with him.

Tapping her combadge immediately, Dax called for medical assistance. Rom backed away from the bar, allowing a tray full of drinks to slip from his grasp and crash to the floor. The other patrons gave Morn a wide berth.

Within moments, Bashir arrived with a nurse, both of them carrying medkits. A security team arrived as well.

Odo kept everyone in the bar back—hardly a difficult task under the circumstances. Also, he signaled for his people to assemble near the entrance, so no one else could get in.

The doctor worked rapidly over Morn, taking readings and analyzing them on his tricorder. The nurse took readings of the glass Morn had used. Then Bashir glanced at Dax, looking a little pale himself.

Not a good sign, the Trill told herself. Not a good sign at all.

"Julian?" she prompted.

Bashir frowned. "We have a new problem, I'm afraid. Morn has the disease. It's on the station."

Worse, Morn wasn't a Bajoran—which meant that, for the first time, the Wrath of the Prophets was crossing species. And that, thought Dax, was the worst sign of all.

She was still thinking it when the lights went out.

As soon as Calculanthra entered the gaming den, he sought out the Ferengi with his eyes. It turned out not to be an easy task.

He turned to Nodogascur, his second cousin on his mother's side. "Where is the little slug?"

Nodogascur pointed to a crowd that had assembled around the dabo table. "Over there," he said. "You can't see him, but he's in there—believe me."

Loath to believe anything, even when it came from his second cousin on his mother's side, Calculanthra made his way through the gaming den. Most of the gamers recognized him and gave way. Those who didn't were shoved aside.

After all, Calculanthra was large and powerful, even for an Orion. One didn't have to know him to know it was prudent to avoid him.

Just as he arrived on the perimeter of the crowd surrounding the dabo table, he heard a cry go up. It was a familiar one, though perhaps not as familiar to Calculanthra personally as he would have liked.

"Dabo!"

"Don't be shy," came a distinctly Ferengi voice. "Step up and make your side bets. I may be on an unbelievable roll, but everyone's bound to fall sometime—am I right?"

There was a chorus of agreement, followed by a flurry of eager betting. Calculanthra pushed in closer, until he could see the Ferengi at the center of it all. Nodogascur was right behind him.

"Is that him?" Calculanthra asked.

His cousin nodded. "That's him, all right. His name is Quark."

Calculanthra sized up the Ferengi—a moment's work. He was just as small and slimy-looking as the rest of his race.

"And you say he's the one who's been asking about the replicators? The ones we sold to that Bajoran?"

Nodogascur nodded again. "That's right. And since we last spoke, I've discovered something more about him. Remember those slave women you wanted? The ones who were bought off the block by the Moborite?"

Maintaining his scrutiny of the Ferengi, Calculanthra grunted. "I remember them too well."

It was no secret how much he had wanted those women, the pick of a wealthy family that had fallen on hard times. The fact that their father had been his rival would have made the acquisition that much sweeter.

"What of it?" he asked Nodogascur.

"It seems," said his cousin, "the Moborites were only a front. This Ferengi was the one who really acquired them. He runs a drinking establishment on a space station, and he wanted some Orions to spice up his business."

Calculanthra felt the anger building inside him. "Then *he* was the one who deprived me of my prize."

"And now he has the gall to come to Mephil Trantos, looking for replicators." Nodogascur chuckled. "But that is not the best part."

"Oh no?" Calculanthra asked, the muscles working in his temples.

"Apparently," his cousin went on, "he arrived in a Federation vessel—with a human at his side. And the human has been seeking the source of the replicators as well."

"How interesting," Calculanthra remarked. "How very interesting indeed." His mouth twisted in an expression of hatred. "I want the Ferengi shown some Orion hospitality—the human as well." He eyed Nodogascur. "You understand me, Cousin?"

Nodogascur smiled with anticipation. "As clearly as ever," he replied.

"Good," Calculanthra said.

He allowed himself a smile. From this point on, the two newcomers were marked men. And around Mephil Trantos, where there was always someone looking to make a quick hundred credits, marked men didn't stay on their feet for very long.

Dax convened a meeting in the wardroom about an hour after Bashir detected the disease in Morn. O'Brien, Odo, and Bashir were seated around the table—not the full complement of trusted friends and competent officers, but it was all she had.

The Trill felt how battered they were emotionally. After all, she was battered, too.

"In case you were wondering," she began, "we still haven't heard anything from either Captain Sisko or Major Kira. But we're hoping that'll change—and soon." She turned to Odo. "What have you learned?"

The shapeshifter grunted. "Apparently, Morn was part of the crew that serviced Kai Winn's craft when the Kai visited a few days back. Someone on her staff must have been carrying the disease."

"And our bio-filters didn't catch it?" Dax asked.

Bashir shook his head. "They're Cardassian, remember—not as sophisticated as the Federation variety."

The Trill accepted that. Turning to O'Brien, she asked, "What about these power fluxes?"

The chief shrugged, clearly caught in the throes of frustration. "My crews have been fixing them as they come up—but we can't seem to find the root of the problem. Anyway, the bar's up and running again."

"Well," Dax said, "from now on, you won't have to do my work as well as yours, Mr. O'Brien. I promise."

She meant it, too. She just wasn't sure she could deliver on it. Right now, her head was pretty clear, pretty focused—but she didn't know when she'd fall victim to another bout of absent-mindedness.

The chief looked at her. "I didn't mean to imply—"

"I know," she said, cutting him off. "But you don't have to imply it. Everyone's seen it for themselves."

Finally she turned to the doctor. "What's the prognosis, Julian?"

He sighed. "Not a brilliant one. Morn's biochemistry is no further from a Bajoran's than mine or yours. So, in theory, if he can be affected—"

"So can everyone else," Odo finished for him.

The doctor nodded. "At this point, I'd have to say everyone's at risk—though it may take longer for some races to be affected than others."

"There's a rumor that Kai Winn has come down with it," the changeling remarked.

"Entirely possible," Bashir replied, "though I haven't heard that one myself."

Odo glanced at Dax. "What do we do about the population on the station? Confirm what they already know from the rumors?"

The Trill pondered the question—but only for a moment. "We have to tell them," she decided. "After all, they're going to find out in any case. Now that there's been an outbreak on the station, we've got to quarantine the place—slap a halt on all ships approaching *Deep Space Nine* and inform the captains docked here that we can't let them leave."

The shapeshifter harrumphed. "I expect there will be some disagreement with that policy. I'll prepare my security officers for that eventuality."

"Good," Dax said. "I've also put a call in to Starfleet for priority medical help. Unfortunately, we're so far off the normal spacelanes, it'll be another two days before help can arrive."

"By then," Bashir noted, "the entire station may be afflicted—humans, Bajorans, Ferengi, everyone."

O'Brien had been slowly sipping his coffee, not saying a thing. But Dax could tell from his expression that he was worried. What's more, she knew why.

Keiko and Molly were down on Bajor. And if the Wrath could affect humans now . . .

Suddenly the chief stood up. "If you'll excuse me," he said, "I've got a call to make." A moment later, he was gone.

The Trill looked at the doctor, then at Odo. "I guess that's all," she told them.

Kira Nerys was awakened by the scream of Ro Laren.

The major was confused, disoriented, and the cry of her companion did nothing to ground her. The floor beneath her was thick with old straw and sawdust, and it was all she could do not to sneeze.

Kira heard, sensed, a body being thrown to the ground near her. And there was a clang . . . the sound of a heavy metal door being slammed. Kira, who was flat on the ground, rolled over—to see that Ro was on her back, slowly sitting up.

"Are you okay?" the major asked.

Ro didn't even look at her.

"I said, are you ok—"

And now Ro did turn to face her, with a look of granite. There was a severe cut on her face. "How sweet of you to care," she said brusquely.

"We have to get that cut cleaned up," Kira said, "or it could get infected."

"Great idea," Ro said. "Let's clean it off with some water . . . oh, but of course, the water in this region is contaminated. And in case you haven't noticed, they've taken away our supplies. Our bottled water, our everything."

"Listen," Kira shot back, "I wasn't looking for this any more than you were."

She was busy inspecting their immediate surroundings. There wasn't much to inspect. It was a windowless room, ten feet by ten. She fancied that it stank of fear, and she wondered what had happened to its previous occupants.

"No, you weren't looking for this, and that's the problem," Ro said. "You're so accustomed to your nice tidy world of *Deep Space Nine,* where everybody kowtows to Major Kira Nerys, you weren't remotely prepared to deal with people who don't give a damn about Bajoran rank, Starfleet connections, or anything else you use to impress people."

That wasn't fair, thought the major. It was a low blow, even for Ro.

"You," she said, stabbing a finger at the Maquis, "know nothing about me. Nothing about *Deep Space Nine,* about my world, about . . . anything. So if you don't have anything intelligent to say, just keep your mouth shut."

Ro turned away from her and leaned with her back against the wall. The two women were silent for a time. The Maquis dabbed at the bleeding on her cheek, putting pressure against it.

Then Kira heard something from nearby. Noises. Street noises—people walking, laughing. The unmistakable reverberations of sound in open air.

"We're not at the bunker," Kira realized. "I didn't think this room looked familiar anyway. They've moved us. This is some sort of holding facility . . . except I don't know what they're holding us for."

"Slave auction," Ro said tonelessly. "It's held about a block or two from here, at a hangout called 'the Place.' They'll be coming for us shortly to add us to the slave pool, I imagine."

"The hell they will." Kira studied Ro's injury from across the room. "How did you get cut, anyway?" she asked.

Ro grunted. "I played up to the guard outside the door. I saw the way he was looking at me." She indicated a small barred window set into the door.

"Thought I could use that. Thought I could then catch him by surprise and make a break for it." She shrugged. "Thought wrong. We wrestled, but he wrestled better than me and tossed me back in here. Sliced me with the knife he kept in his belt."

Kira frowned. "You should have waited for me to wake up. Maybe together we could have—"

"Together?" Ro snorted derisively. "Since when have we been together in this? It's been the Kira Nerys show, guest-starring Ro Laren. You've made it quite clear just how much input you want from me."

"Okay, fine," Kira said impatiently. "So here's where we stand. I led the charge to the bunker, still clinging to a false belief that at least some of the people I came into contact with were dealing on the up-and-up. And you tried to stage your own private break-out while I was unconscious, and all you got was injured for your efforts."

The Maquis shook her head. "That's not all I got."

"Oh? What else?"

"Well," Ro said, "considering he had a knife in his belt, I didn't think that he would particularly miss the one in his boot." And she held up a fairly nasty-looking blade.

Kira gaped in surprise. "How did you—?"

"When he shoved me to the ground, I noticed a hilt peeking out of his boot. As he kicked me back into the cell, I snatched it." She smiled grimly. "What I figure is, sooner or later, they're going to have to come in here to get us—to transfer us to the Place. And when they do—"

"And when they do, armed with only a knife and our good looks, we take down however many people are sent in here," Kira said skeptically. "People who in turn might be armed with who-knows-what. Great plan there."

"You have a better idea?" Ro asked. Then she rolled her eyes. "Why do I even ask?"

CHAPTER
10

KAI WINN PACED her temple, rubbing the sides of her forehead and trying to remove the pain that pounded within her. There had to be answers. Somewhere, there had to be answers.

Had they truly strayed so far that they were irredeemable? Was the situation on Bajor utterly hopeless?

The numbers were brought to her every hour. The number of dead. The number of reported new cases. The Wrath of the Prophets had spread with hideous velocity, like a ravenous fire scorching every life in its path.

She had prayed; oh, how she had prayed. She had meditated, she had offered supplications, she had studied ancient texts to search for precedents and how they were handled. Whenever she was not praying, she was studying, and vice versa—night and day, neglecting herself, until she couldn't remember the last time she'd slept more than an hour or so.

Winn consulted one of her books and began murmuring the invocations in it, although reading wasn't really necessary. After all this time, she had the invocation seared into her memory.

She spoke faster and faster, words tripping one over the other, and then she began to realize that the words didn't seem to have any meaning to her anymore—if indeed they ever had. They were just . . . just sounds. Random syllables, noises that bore no relationship to anything real.

Her throat was raw from all her praying, and she swirled her tongue over her cracked lips. She was thirsty. She was thirsty a lot lately, but she'd ignored it just as she'd ignored everything else. . . .

Suddenly she threw the prayer book down. It crashed to the floor and she shouted to the heavens, "What do you want from us? What do you want? To kill us all? Is that it? Just . . . just cut us down, like excess wheat? Is this just some exercise in cruelty? What did we do to deserve this? What could anyone do to deserve this?"

Her voice was rising higher in pitch, and higher still, until it began to sound like a screech. "Are we actually supposed to worship you? Give thanks when you provide us with favors, and tremble and beg for forgiveness when you inflict some new hardship on us?

"Is that how you wish to rule over us? With fear? Don't you know anything? Even the lowliest mortal can tell you it's far better to be respected because of love than because of fear. How can we know this simple fact while you, the Prophets, are oblivious to it?"

She began to cough violently, her rage not yet spent. "For years, decades, I preached your word. I condemned those who did not believe, and I fought back against the impious and the impure. We've tried our best—we are not perfect. We can never be perfect. But, Prophets, we deserve better than this! We deserve . . ."

The room began to spin around her, and a new fit of coughing seized her. She put her hand to her mouth, drew her palm away, and saw it tinged with blood.

"We deserve better," she whispered, and then she collapsed.

And the count of those who had been afflicted with the plague increased by one.

"So?" Sisko asked.

Quark frowned. "Nothing *yet.*"

They were on their way back to the quarters they'd rented on Mephil Trantos. So far, neither of them had been able to find out a thing about the smuggling operation or the source of the replicators. And time was running out for the Bajorans.

"Still," the Ferengi went on, "I think I'm getting close. Another couple of days and our luck might change."

"It's changed already," said someone up ahead, from beyond the point where the corridor jogged left.

A moment later, the owner of the voice showed himself. And much to the captain's chagrin, he wasn't alone.

There were four of them altogether. And unfortunately for Sisko and Quark, they didn't look anything like the welcome wagon.

Given the poor lighting, it was difficult to see their individual features. However, one was so big and broad he could only have been a Pandrilite.

Another resembled a warrior-caste Skelarian, if his thick torso and his protuberant eyeballs were any indication. The third one could have been a Rythrian, judging from his considerable height and the loose flaps of skin that served as ears.

The fourth one, Sisko couldn't even guess at. He looked like a mess of angles, with black leathery skin that hung on his bones like a suit in Garak's tailor shop. But his hands and feet were each twice the size of the average human's, and he probably wasn't the least bit shy about using them.

The captain wondered why the four weren't armed. At least, not obviously so. Then he came up with the answer all by himself.

Their employer didn't want them dead—not yet, anyway. He wanted to be be able to question them first. *Then* he would kill them.

"Are we in trouble?" Quark whispered to him.

"That depends," the captain replied.

"On what?" asked the Ferengi.

"On whether you mind getting beaten within an inch of your life."

Quark swallowed. It was a sound even a deaf man could've heard.

"Do you think it would do any good to reason with them?" he asked.

"Do *you?*" Sisko answered.

The Ferengi snuck a look at him. "I thought Starfleet captains *always* tried to reason with their enemies."

The human grunted. "Report me to Starfleet Command."

Then there was no more time to talk. Their antagonists were coming at them with an obvious desire to inflict bodily harm. Or rather, coming at Sisko alone, because Quark had suddenly vanished from his side.

The only aspect of the situation that worked in the captain's favor was the narrowness of the corridor, which prevented all four of his attackers from seizing him at the same time. As luck would have it, the Rythrian and the Skelarian wound up in the front line.

Sisko waited until they were almost on top of him, then pulled back his foot and let it fly. It caught the alien square in the belly—for all the good it did. Skelarians were known for their ability to withstand physical trauma, and this one was no exception.

Before the captain could quite regain his balance, the Rythrian was swinging at him. Sisko barely had time to twist backward out of the way—and watch his adversary's fist slam into the hard unyielding wall.

The Rythrian yelped with pain and clutched his wounded hand. A moment later, the captain connected with a well-placed uppercut, snapping the Rythrian's head back and knocking him senseless.

Then it was the Skelarian's turn again—or it would have been, if things had gone according to Sisko's expectations. But before he could aim another kick, he saw Quark scurry out of nowhere and attach himself to the alien's leg.

The Skelarian grabbed Quark by his shoulders and tried to pull him off, but no one was more tenacious than a scared-to-death Ferengi. When the alien opened his mouth and roared in his deep bass voice, the captain knew Quark's teeth were as sharp as ever.

Taking advantage of the timely assistance, Sisko took a couple of steps backward and launched himself into the air. This time, when he lashed out with his foot, it was with a good deal more power than before.

Of course, the captain wasn't aiming at the Skelarian. It would take more than a single kick to bring a specimen like *him* down.

No, he was aiming for the hulking Pandrilite in back of the Skelarian. What's more, his kick was right on target. It caught the Pandrilite square in the solar plexus, delivering an impact that knocked the breath out of him.

Gasping like a fish out of water, the Pandrilite sunk to his knees. Just for good measure, Sisko slammed him into the wall.

Then it was him and the fourth alien. Up close, the captain suddenly realized whom he was dealing with.

But before the knowledge could do him any good, he felt something hard catch him on the side of the head, staggering him.

Sisko tried to anticipate the follow-up blow, but it came too quickly to avoid altogether. It slammed him in the left shoulder, numbing his arm down to his fingertips. The third blow sent him reeling.

A Denebian, he thought, as he hit the base of the wall and slid to the floor. *A damned Denebian.* It had to be. No one else could strike that quickly.

But he'd always heard that Denebians *hated* Orions. It was just his luck to find the one that *didn't*.

As the captain tried to gather his feet beneath him, he saw the Denebian coming at him for another round. From all indications, it wouldn't be much of a contest.

Still, Sisko wasn't about to throw in the towel. As the alien came for him, he feigned dizziness—then swung his leg out at the last second, hoping to sweep the Denebian's legs out from under him.

It didn't work. It didn't even come close to working. The alien simply skipped over the captain's leg and launched a kick of his own. Sisko tried to sidestep and deflect the kick with his good arm. But he failed. Miserably.

It struck him in the side. *Hard.* So hard, in fact, that he felt a couple of ribs crack.

The pain took his breath away. His mind told him to roll out of harm's way, to save himself from the next assault as best he could—and then he felt himself lifted by his tunic from behind. He didn't have to turn around to know the Rythrian had recovered from his mishap.

"You're going to regret what you did to me!" the alien snapped, his voice seething with anger.

No doubt, he was right. The captain had only to see the way the Denebian was pulling back his fist to make that determination. He could almost feel the impact already.

And the Denebian had barely warmed up. This wasn't going to be pleasant, he told himself.

"Hold it right there!" came a familiar voice.

Sisko turned, though it cost him a shot of pain in his tortured ribs. Despite everything, he smiled. How could he help it?

For there was Quark, standing over the prone figure of the Skelarian. And bless his bulbous little head, he had a phaser in each hand. One was pointed at the Denebian, the other at the Rythrian.

The captain felt himself released by his captor—a good thing, but also a bad one considering his injury. As he made jarring impact with the floor, he felt as if someone had prodded him in the side with a hot poker.

"He's not fast enough to take us both down," hissed the Rythrian. He was referring to the Ferengi, of course.

"I beg to differ," Quark said, the picture of confidence.

Sisko didn't expect they'd take his word for it. In the next fraction of a second, both of his antagonists went for their weapons.

The captain only had time to spoil one adversary's aim. Unfortunately, the Rythrian was the closer of the two. Lashing out with his foot, he slammed his heel into the alien's ankle. The Rythrian's shot went awry, missing Sisko's ally by nearly a meter.

But by then, Quark and the Denebian had already fired, their respective blasts of tightly focused energy crisscrossing savagely in the corridor's narrow confines. For a moment, in the silence that followed, the captain wasn't sure exactly what had happened.

Then the Denebian fell to his knees, made a loud sighing sound, and pitched forward onto his face. Despite all his speed, the Ferengi had nailed him.

The Rythrian cursed loudly and volubly. Obviously, *he* couldn't figure it out *either*. Slumping against the wall to take his weight off his damaged ankle, he took aim at Quark a second time.

But the Ferengi had him dead to rights. Depressing the trigger mechanism on his phaser, Quark blasted the Rythrian in the chest—knocking him over the Pandrilite, who was just starting to get up off the floor.

Then he trained his weapon on the Pandrilite as well. One more lurid red beam, one more grunt, one more unconscious alien.

Sisko turned to the Ferengi, making no attempt to disguise his admiration. "Where in hell did you learn to do *that?*" he asked.

The Ferengi looked at him, making an all-too-obvious attempt to feign puzzlement. "Do what?" he asked.

Sisko frowned and pointed at one of the phasers in

Quark's hands. "Do *that,*" he replied, playing the game.

Quark looked down at the weapons as if seeing them for the first time. His brow creased. "You know," he said, "I haven't the slightest idea."

Sisko grunted. "I'm sure you don't," he remarked cynically.

Bracing himself against the wall, the captain got to his feet with an effort. The pain must have shown on his face.

"What's wrong?" asked the Ferengi, with what seemed like real concern.

"Nothing I can't handle," Sisko informed him, making his way along the wall toward his companion.

"Don't give me that," Quark said, tilting his head to get a better look at the captain. "You're hurt. I don't need Dr. Bashir to tell me when someone's cracked a few of his ribs."

"It's not as bad as it looks," Sisko insisted.

"You'd better hope not," the Ferengi remarked, wincing sympathetically. "If it were, I'd be offering you a brochure on a variety of lovely burial sites." He paused. "Where do think you're going, anyway?"

Now within a half-meter of Quark, Sisko reached out and grabbed one of the Ferengi's borrowed phasers. "I *think* I'm going to commandeer one of *these,*" he explained.

"Ah," said the Ferengi. "I see. You know, I could have just handed it to you, if you'd simply asked for it."

"I didn't want to inconvenience you," the captain replied.

He straightened experimentally. The pain didn't get any worse as a result—a good sign, in his estimation.

"Incidentally," he said, casting a look back at Quark. "What did you do to the Skelarian?"

The Ferengi shrugged. "I worked on a Ferengi freighter for a while. There was a Skelarian aboard. You could say we didn't like each other. And since he was a lot bigger than I was, I had to find his weak point."

"Which was?" Sisko asked, as he made his way back toward the fallen aliens.

"If you want to know *that,*" Quark said, "you'll have to pay for the information, the same way *I* did. So are you going to interrogate one of these fine specimens? Find out why they came after us?"

"That's what the phaser is for," the captain explained.

Kneeling beside the Rythrian, who seemed the least likely to resist a show of force, Sisko pointed his weapon at the alien's face. Then he slapped the Rythrian lightly on the cheek with the back of his hand.

The alien stirred. His eyes fluttered open.

He saw the human.

He saw the human's phaser.

He swallowed.

"What is it you want?" he asked.

"You know what I want," Sisko told him. "The identity of the one who hired you—who he is and why he wanted us."

The Rythrian swallowed again. He didn't take his eyes off the captain's weapon. "And if I don't want to tell you?" he inquired, aspiring to bravado.

Sisko smiled, despite the searing pain in his side. "Then I'll just get it from one of your playmates. Your corpse will show them how serious I am."

That was all it took to make the alien a veritable font of useful information.

Zeber was beginning to be sorry he had asked for guard detail this time around.

Under normal circumstances, Zeber liked coming along to the auctions in Sorshaq. The women up on the block were often scantily clad. And the ones he was guarding would, occasionally, be so desperate to try and break free that, well . . . things could go well for him. He never let them go, of course, but desperation could be a great motivator.

The Bajoran, however, had not exactly been cooperative. He hadn't intended to cut her; in fact, he was worried Manimoujak was going to be angry with him. No one liked merchandise that was damaged.

Still, the cut was a fairly superficial one, and she could be cleaned up and patched with no outward sign of a problem. It's not as if he had sliced off something she was going to need later on.

Then Zeber noticed that the arguing between the two Bajorans was getting louder again. They'd been making some sort of noise in their cell before, but it had tapered off.

Now they were at it again. Words were being flung around in heated fashion, each of them accusing each other of all manner of things.

"That is stupid!" one of them was saying. He recognized the voice as that of the one he'd injured. Ro, her name had been. "That is no kind of escape plan! There is no way in hell that's going to work!"

"It's just like you to give up and say there's no hope!"

"There *is* no hope! It's all your fault, you stupid rinta. If it weren't for you, everything would be fine! But now everything is screwed up, and there's nothing you can do about it!"

"I'm warning you," said the other prisoner, and her voice really sounded on edge. "I have absolutely had it with you! So help me, one more word—"

Ro supplied the word. In fact, she supplied several.

And then she shrieked, a cry of pure terror. Zeber, who'd been lazily leaning against the door, heard the shout, followed by a loud thud. He peered in through the window of the door.

The other Bajoran was withdrawing from Ro. And Ro was on the floor, flopping around like a just-landed fish, trying to extract . . .

A knife. Zeber gasped. There was a knife in her chest, buried almost up to the hilt. She was gasping, whimpering, and there was blood trickling from her mouth.

Zeber could only imagine his boss's fury. He

yanked open the door and whipped out his disruptor, aiming it at the other Bajoran.

"Stay back!" he snarled. "Stay right where you are!"

She showed no inclination to move. She just watched him with her dark and glowering eyes.

He crouched next to Ro. "Just . . . just stay calm," he said. "I'll take care of everyth—"

That was as much as he managed to say before Ro suddenly sat up, grabbed his disruptor hand, and shoved it upward. His finger squeezed the trigger reflexively, but it discharged harmlessly overhead.

Before he knew it, the other Bajoran woman was in front of him, driving the heel of her hand in his direction. He felt an impact on the point of his chin, then fell into a deep dark pit of unconsciousness.

Kira surveyed her handiwork. The guard was out cold, sprawled on the straw of their cell.

Ro sat up, tossing aside the remains of the knife . . . the knife that she'd broken off just above the hilt, so it could effectively look as if the rest of the blade had been sunk into her chest.

"Now that was the performance of a lifetime," she murmured.

"How did you bleed out of your mouth?" Kira asked.

"Bit down on my lip and inner cheek. It's going to swell a bit, but it's nothing I can't live with."

"Well," said the major, "you scared the hell out of me when I saw that, and I knew what was going on."

Ro wiped away the blood. Her face was already

starting to look slightly puffy. She extended a hand to Kira and said, "Help me up?"

For the first time in any of her dealings with Ro Laren, Kira did not hesitate. She took Ro's hand firmly and pulled her to her feet.

As they emerged from their cell, they heard footfalls. No doubt, they belonged to whoever was going to escort them to the auction facility.

Kira flattened against a wall and cradled her weapon. So did Ro. Then they waited.

CHAPTER
11

THE PLACE WAS more crowded than usual, Manimoujak reflected. But then, it was always crowded when there was a slave auction on the schedule.

It was held in the back room, as usual. Actually, the back room was almost as large as the interior of the Place itself. It had to be, to accommodate the usual hordes of both buyers and onlookers.

The crush of typical Sorshaq lowlifes and reprobates spread into the room like a fungal infection. There was a podium up front where the slaves were supposed to be brought up, one by one, for viewing and bidding.

Sandon, the bartender, had taken the job of auctioneer for himself, leaving the backup bartender at the front while he attended to the business in the back. Looking over an audience packed with Bajorans, Orions, Yridians, Tellarites, Andorians, and others, he called out, "As always, bidding will be in gold-pressed latinum! We're not exactly in a position to accept credit." This generated a couple of guffaws from the crowd.

The slaves were being huddled together in a pen located at one end of the room. From his vantage point some ten meters away, Manimoujak studied the frightened assemblage of property.

He frowned and turned to one of his men. "Where are those two Bajoran women? I sent Tobar and Wiley over to fetch them. What's taking them so long?"

"I'll check on them," his aide said, and hurried off.

A familiar face caught Manimoujak's attention. "Gnome," he called.

Gnome sidled through the crowd and drew near to Manimoujak. "Good to see you," Gnome said.

"I should have known you'd be here," Manimoujak replied. "You never miss one, do you?"

"Well," Gnome said, "I've got a personal stake in this." He pointed to the slave pen. "See that one?"

Manimoujak looked at a Bajoran woman, who appeared to be just shy of twenty. She was half-naked and clearly frightened as she huddled with the other slaves in the holding pen.

"What about her, Gnome?"

"That, my friend, is Varis Sul, tetrarch of the Paqu village. I had"—he framed the word distastefully—"a *dealing* with her. She slipped away from me and stole my ship to boot. If she'd had the brains to stay put in her village, she would have been safe. I wouldn't have bothered with her. But she came back out, started poking around some more . . . and a longtime associate of mine was kind enough to steer her right into my hands."

"Payback is truly a joyous thing," acknowledged Manimoujak.

At that moment, Sandon set the festivities into motion. "Our first item," he called, "had been intended as a set—a fine Bajoran male and his son. However, we've had several inquiries about breaking up the pair, since there are some who are interested in the boy but not the father. We are happy to accommodate all reasonable requests, and so . . ."

He snapped his fingers, and his men reached into the pen and began to drag the boy out. He shrieked for his father, clutched at him, and his father tried to lunge forward. Prods were produced by Sandon's men and the father was jolted back, falling into the arms of Varis Sul, as the boy was hoisted up onto the stage.

"Now," Sandon called, "who will start the bidding . . ." And then his nose wrinkled.

There was a new aroma added to the smell of the Place. A very distinctive, very frightening aroma.

An aroma that was confirmed a moment later when the right side of the room suddenly erupted in flame. It was as if someone had soaked it in alcohol and set it ablaze.

Which was, as Manimoujak would learn later, exactly what someone had done.

"Fire!" Sandon shrieked, but he was somewhat late

in the announcement. Already there were shouts of fear, stampeding feet, and jostling among the attendees, as they sought a way out of what had become a death trap.

And the way was quickly provided as the far wall blew open, rocked by an explosion. It sounded as if someone had discovered Sandon's hidden cache of explosives in one of the side rooms, wired the exterior wall, and blown that side of the building sky-high.

Which was, as Manimoujak would also learn, exactly what someone had done.

With the fire spreading at alarming speed, the entire Place—both front and back rooms—emptied out. The only occupants not accounted for were the intended slaves, who stood within the confines of their enclosure and shook the bars, screeching to be let out. But no one listened or cared.

The flight of the customers carried them out into the labyrinthine side alleys. Manimoujak and Gnome charged down one of them . . . only to skid to a halt.

Running toward them, a disruptor in her hand, was Ro Laren. Her eyes narrowing, she fired at them. Somehow, they managed to avoid the resulting disruptor blast.

Then Gnome, moving with startling speed, came at her. But Ro whirled, and suddenly she was holding a knife that whipped across Gnome's upper chest. He let out a high-pitched yelp and backpedaled, taking a header over a trash can.

Ro looked as if she was going to inflict even more damage. But fortunately for Manimoujak—and

Gnome—a section of flaming ceiling fell in front of her, screening them from view. Taking advantage of it, they fled, heading down a connecting alley and putting as much distance between themselves and the Place as they could.

Kira Nerys was in the middle of the inferno. Like a salmon fighting upstream, she had shoved her way into the room and was working on prying open the cage that held the prospective slaves.

"Hurry!" they were shouting. "Hurry!"

"Stand back!" she said, and pulled out a disruptor. She fired once at the lock and it blasted free of the enclosure. "Okay!" she yelled. "Come on! Let's go! Move! Move!"

With the father scooping up his son, the lot of them tore out of their prison. Ro poked her head through the hole they'd made in the wall, gesturing for them to hurry through. Smoke billowed behind the prisoners as they made their exit.

"You sure took your sweet time!" Kira shouted at her as she brought up the rear.

Suddenly someone grabbed her by the foot, sending her crashing to the floor. She rolled over just in time to see the slave-barker lunging at her, a jagged bottle in his hand and murder in his heart.

Kira barely managed to roll out of the way as the bottle shattered against the floor next to her. She drove a foot up, caught the barker in the pit of the stomach, and sent him stumbling back.

"You idiot!" she cried. "The place is burning!"

"It's my place! You've ruined my place!" he howled.

"Kira, get out of there!" Ro shouted through the smoke.

The major couldn't see her. The smoke was too thick—which meant Ro probably couldn't see her either. And even if she could, she'd have been crazy to risk her life doing it.

Apparently Kira was on her own.

The barker came at her like a man possessed. Obviously he wasn't thinking clearly, and there wasn't going to be enough time to wait for him to come to his senses.

Heat billowed over Kira and she staggered back, firing her disruptor blindly. Her adversary ducked in under it, knocking into her arm and sending the shot high.

The blast struck a part of the ceiling that hadn't fallen yet. Huge flaming chunks of debris rained down on the slave-barker, crushing him instantly. Instinctively Kira took a step forward to try and help him, but she knew it was too late.

Then a hand grabbed her by the wrist. She turned and, through the smoke, saw Ro. The Maquis got hold of Kira's arm and pulled her toward the hole in the wall—which, in all the smoke and flames, Kira might not have been able to find on her own.

They ran from the Place, then heard a crashing sound. They stopped and turned in time to see the entire establishment collapse in on itself, a swarm of embers rising from the impact.

"All right," Ro said finally. "Now what?"

Kira pulled in draft after draft of the clean air. "Looking to me for a decision? I'm honored."

The Maquis grunted. "I didn't say I'd be bound by it; I just wanted to know if you had any thoughts."

"Now," Kira said, "we go back after Manimoujak."

"Good thought," Ro agreed. "We went there once to try and find out what he knows about this disease. I think a second visit will prove more fruitful."

The major nodded. "Me, too."

The two women looked at each other. Both of them were smeared with soot, except where trails of sweat had made their way down the sides of their faces.

"This is beginning to frighten me a little," Kira said.

"You mean that we're thinking alike." Ro frowned. "Same here."

Then they heard a ragged voice speak up behind them, and they spun as one, bringing weapons up to bear. But all they targeted was a young Bajoran woman.

"One of the slaves," Ro murmured.

Kira sighed. "You can go," she said. "You're free. Get out of here, as fast and as far as your legs will take you."

But the slave wouldn't budge. "I'm Varis Sul," she said, "and I'm going with you."

Suddenly Kira recognized the woman. "Of course. I

remember you. I'm sorry, I didn't recognize you at first."

"I have looked better," Varis admitted ruefully.

Kira, by way of explanation, turned to Ro and said, "She's the tetrarch. The one from the Paqu village. The one who—"

Ro glanced at Varis. "Who started this, yes."

"We don't know that for sure," Kira countered.

For some reason, she felt compelled to say something to this poor, disheveled young woman who clearly carried the weight of the world—or at least the health of the world—on her shoulders.

"It could have been a setup. It could have—"

"How did you get here?" Ro asked the tetrarch.

Varis shook her head. "I asked the wrong questions of the wrong people, and was looking in the wrong direction at the wrong time."

Kira and Ro exchanged glances.

"I can sympathize," said the major.

"Then sympathize with this," Varis told her. "I'm coming with you."

Kira smiled. "No, you're not."

The tetrarch's eyes burned with fury, and when she spoke it was with such anger her body trembled. "I will see this through," she said. "I will make up for the grief I have caused, and I will strike back at those who have injured my planet and myself. And I will do this whether you want me to or not, so you might as well want me to."

Kira saw in Varis Sul all the fire, all the passion she

had had in her own youth. The major had been traveling the length and breadth of Bajor, looking for signs of the dedication and vehemence of the old days. She had looked for them in those who had been her allies. And she had found them all wanting.

But this girl . . . this young woman, who stood before them like one large clenched fist . . . she had it. She was, Kira felt, the incarnation of what Bajor was supposed to be.

After finally finding what she was searching for, how could the major turn away now?

She looked to see if Ro was entertaining similar thoughts, but the Maquis was just shaking her head. The word *no* was already forming on her lips.

"All right, fine," Kira said, "but watch your back." She headed off down the street, with Varis Sul right behind her. Ro was left standing there, scratching her head. Clearly she was wondering if she was ever going to understand anything Kira Nerys did.

"Look," Quark said, "you don't have to do this."

But before the words had entirely left his mouth, he knew that there would be no stopping his companion. Sisko looked as determined as the Ferengi had ever seen him as he made his way along the corridor toward the gaming room.

"But we already know Calculanthra's the source of the replicators," Quark argued. "Can't we figure out the rest when we get back?"

The captain glanced at him. "You know we can't.

We need to know where the damned things came from. And we need the name of the Bajoran he dealt with—the middle man who actually arranged for the replicators' delivery. Don't think for even a moment that we're leaving this place without them."

Quark scurried ahead, turned, and blocked Sisko's path. "But we've obviously overstayed our welcome here," he insisted. "And you, with a couple of broken ribs—what good will you be against a roomful of thieves and cutthroats? Isn't it better to go home and consolidate our gains?"

"You're talking like a Ferengi," the captain snapped, slowing down.

"I *am* a Ferengi," Quark pointed out.

"That's no excuse," Sisko said. "Now move aside."

But the Ferengi wouldn't budge. "All right," he declared. "If you're so intent on barging in there and getting your head blown off, that's fine. Far be it from me to keep you from a good time." He held up his hands in an appeal for rational thought. "Just do me one favor. If the going gets rough, let me handle it. After all, I know how these people think."

The captain looked at Quark for a moment, as if trying to divine his intent. Then he muttered a curse under his breath.

"I must be delirious," the captain said, "but I'm going to trust you. Just this once. And so help me, if I see you do *anything* that smacks of a mercantile transaction . . ."

He held up his phaser for effect, obviously ignoring

the fact that the Ferengi was still in possession of one of his own. Quark nodded, a gesture meant to put Sisko's fears to rest.

"Don't worry," he remarked. "I give you my word of honor I'll practice restraint."

Sisko frowned. "Now I feel *much* better."

"My word of honor as a *businessman,*" Quark amended.

The captain sighed. "If that's the best you can do . . ."

"Then it's a deal," the Ferengi blurted. "Er . . . I mean, we're agreed."

"We're agreed," Sisko echoed.

"Good," Quark said, stepping aside so the captain could go by.

Now all he had to do was figure out a way for both of them to come out of this alive. He didn't expect that to be any more difficult than, oh, say, getting a Vulcan to crack a smile.

On the other hand, he conceded, *this* might be more fun.

Sisko's first problem, as he entered the gaming den, was that he had a name—Calculanthra—but he had no idea which Orion went with the name. He addressed the problem as quickly and economically as he could.

By shouting "Calculanthra!" out loud, as if it were a challenge—which, in effect, it was.

Beside the captain, Quark cringed. Clearly, direct confrontation wasn't his favorite tactic.

Everyone in the room turned his or her head to look at the human. For a moment, no one moved. No one responded to the challenge.

Then an Orion came forward. A godawful *big* Orion at that.

"I'm Calculanthra," he replied, his eyes narrowing. "And who in the name of plunder are *you?*"

Sisko walked up to the Orion. Those who stood in his way got out of it. If there was a fight, they clearly didn't want any part of it.

By that sign alone, the captain should have known he was in over his head. But he wasn't going to let that stop him. Not when there were millions of Bajoran lives at stake.

When he was toe to toe with Calculanthra, he looked up at him. The Orion had a good six inches on him. "My name," he said, "is Benjamin Sisko—the same Benjamin Sisko you sent your thugs after. By the way, you can scrape them off the bulkheads anytime now. And before you ask, I'll tell you I'm here to find out about the replicators—the ones you smuggled into Bajor."

Calculanthra showed him a mouthful of sharpened teeth. "I don't do business with Bajor," he answered.

"That's a lie," the captain said evenly, "and both of us know it. Now let's not waste any more time— yours or mine. As I told you, I want to know where you got those replicators."

The Orion laughed. "Even if I *had* smuggled them into Bajor, you think I'd tell you?"

Sisko drew his phaser out of his tunic and held it to

the underside of Calculanthra's jaw. "I think you might," he replied reasonably.

But the Orion didn't back down. "Look around," he told the captain. "This room is full of my people. You think they're going to let you get away with this? Do you?"

Sisko smiled. "Probably not. But I'll have the satisfaction of knowing I've disposed of you first." He paused. "Then again, neither one of us needs to get hurt. All you have to do is tell me what I want to know."

That's when Quark insinuated himself between the captain and Calculanthra. "Gentlemen, gentlemen," he said, "there's no need for a confrontation. Surely we can settle this some other way."

"I doubt it," the Orion replied. "I don't like having a phaser held to my face."

With a jerk of his head, he signaled to some of his men in the room. Sisko watched them spread out to block the exits.

"But we *can* settle it," the Ferengi insisted. He turned to Calculanthra. "Unless what I've heard about you is untrue."

The Orion eyed him. "And what's that?"

Quark shrugged. "That when it comes to gambling, you've got nerves of titanium." He stopped to think. "Or was it some other part of your anatomy?"

"I've been known to spin the dabo wheel," Calculanthra conceded. "What about it?"

The Ferengi rubbed his hands together. "I've been

174

known to spin it myself. In fact, I've had quite a bit of luck today. Of course, that was a while ago. By now, my luck's probably run out."

The Orion obviously didn't get it. "So?"

Quark frowned. "So I'd like to take our dispute to a higher plane. Instead of beating each other senseless—instead of taking a chance that someone could get killed—I suggest we venture everything on a roll of the dabo wheel."

The captain nodded, seeing where his partner was going with this. "If we win," he told Calculanthra, "you tell us everything we want to know. And we leave scot-free."

The Orion seemed intrigued. "And if I win," he proposed, "the two of you become my slaves—to be sold to the highest bidder."

Sisko wasn't in love with the idea. But before he could say anything about it, Quark clasped Calculanthra's hand. "It's a deal," he confirmed.

The Orion sneered at him. "Good. Let's get started." He glanced meaningfully at the captain.

Reluctantly Sisko lowered his phaser and put it away. He half-expected Calculanthra's men to pounce on him, but they didn't. Apparently, even Orions had some principles.

"Odds," Calculanthra said.

"Evens," the Ferengi countered.

Of course, as even the captain knew, that was just one variation of the game. But given the circumstances, it was the one that made the most sense.

"I'll spin," said the Orion, taking hold of the wheel.

"Not so fast," Quark told him, putting his hand on the wheel as well.

Calculanthra glowered at him. "In a Ferengi bar, you go first. This is Mephil Trantos. Here, *I* go first."

Quark bit his lip, but he didn't argue with the logic. As a result, neither did the captain. He just watched the Orion send the wheel spinning merrily with a flick of his powerful wrist.

At first, the wheel was spinning too quickly for Sisko to see more than a blur. Then, as it slowed, he saw the shiny titanium ball bouncing from one slot to the next.

It landed in an even-numbered slot, then an odd one, then an even again. And the fates of not only the captain and Quark, but that of an entire world, rode with it.

Odd. Even. Odd. Even.

The wheel spun slower and slower. After a while, the titanium ball barely moved. Finally it seemed to come to rest in an odd-numbered slot. Sisko's heart sank in his chest.

Odd meant they lost. In a matter of moments, they'd be Calculanthra's slaves—and Bajor's hopes, already slim, would be dashed altogether.

Then, as if nudged by some kindly fate, the ball roused itself and trickled into the next berth. An *even*-numbered berth.

And that's where it stayed as the wheel lost its momentum. In another few seconds, it came to a halt.

The captain looked up at Calculanthra. "As I said," he began, "I've got some questions. About the source of the replicators. And about the Bajorans involved in bringing them planetside."

The Orion's lip curled and his complexion darkened with anger and resentment—but he didn't protest. Instead, he ushered Sisko and Quark into a quiet corner of the gaming room.

Then, his eyes bulging, he spat out a single word: "Ask."

Sisko asked, all right. And he got at least one of the answers he needed—the identities of the Bajorans involved in the smuggling ring.

But he couldn't find out where the replicators came from. Calculanthra insisted he didn't know that— that he'd bought them from a Tellarite who'd bought them from someone else, and so on down the line.

The captain sighed. If the Orion had decided to hide something, it would've been his contacts on Bajor—and he'd given those away freely. Or if he'd been lying, he could have lied about both things just as easily. So, more than likely, Calculanthra was as ignorant about the replicators as he claimed.

It was Quark who finally signaled an end to the conversation. "Well," he said at last, smiling at the Orion, "thank you for your time and your cooperation. I hope next time, we'll meet under more pleasant circumstances."

He held out his hand to Calculanthra, who looked for all the world as if he were going to bite it off. "If I ever see you around this place again," the Orion growled, "I'll have you killed. No—I'll kill you with my own hands. Is that understood?"

"Too well," the Ferengi replied.

Sisko didn't like being threatened, but they'd already pushed their luck as far as it was likely to go. Besides, they had what they'd come for—and his side hurt like hell.

With a parting glare, he got up and led the way out of the gaming room. Nor was Quark far behind.

Once they were out in the corridor, the captain turned to the Ferengi. "So how did you do it?" he inquired.

"Do what?" Quark asked.

"Fix the dabo wheel."

The Ferengi looked at him. "I didn't," he replied.

Sisko was surprised. "Then how did you know we'd win?"

"I didn't," Quark repeated.

The captain stopped dead in his tracks. "You mean you left our fate entirely to chance?"

"We had a fifty-fifty chance," the Ferengi explained. "Those aren't bad odds under any circumstances. Besides, I had no intention of becoming a slave of the Orions even if we lost. I was going to whip out my phaser and make a break for it."

"Sure you were," Sisko said beneath his breath, resuming his progress down the corridor. It only took him a few strides to catch up with Quark.

"Of course," the Ferengi assured him, "you were in my plans as well. I wasn't about to leave without you." He cleared his throat. "That is, unless I absolutely had to."

"Hard to believe," the captain observed mockingly. "Our very own Quark. A scofflaw and a rulebreaker."

"What's harder to believe," said the Ferengi, "is that Calculanthra took our bargain so much to heart. Usually, it's the old-fashioned Orions who frequent the gaming establishments, and they don't follow *anyone's* rules—even their own."

"All the more reason to get a move on," Sisko noted. "The less time he has to change his mind, the better."

"Good point," Quark agreed, and got his legs churning that much faster.

In fact, with his rib injury making it hard to breathe deeply, the captain had some trouble keeping up. But then, he told himself, there's no being in the cosmos faster than a Ferengi who thinks his life may be in danger.

CHAPTER
12

QUARK LEANED BACK in his seat and surveyed the
Defiant's helm controls. They were well on their way
back to the Bajoran system, having left Mephil Trantos and established contact with *Deep Space Nine* a
good hour ago.

Sisko had been less than overjoyed at having to
report their mixed success, even though they'd established a key link in the smuggling ring that ran from
Orion territory all the way to Bajor. But that hadn't
done the Bajorans any good in the short term. Their
biggest problem was still the virus.

"You've got to admit," Quark said, glancing over
his shoulder at his companion, "things could have
worked out a lot worse. We got what we came for, put
a crimp in Bajor's black market and—"

"And nearly got ourselves killed in the process," the captain commented dryly from his center seat. "More than once, in fact."

"I guess those ribs still smart," the Ferengi observed. He shrugged and turned back to the helm controls. "Well, I'm sure it's nothing Dr. Bashir won't be able to repair."

Behind him, Sisko grunted. "You're all heart, Quark."

"That's what they tell me," the Ferengi replied. He sighed. "Sure was good to get back to my old stomping grounds."

"I'll bet," the human remarked absently.

"Of course," Quark went on, "it would have been even better if those Pandrilite twins had been there. I was told they settled down a couple of years back and bought a theater on Culpidus. Theater in the round, I think they call it." He turned to Sisko again and winked. "If you know what I mean."

The captain rolled his eyes and checked out something or other. Life support, the Ferengi thought, or sensors, or some such drivel. Sisko was always concerning himself with such things, even when it was clearly unnecessary.

"You know," Quark said out loud, "I really like that Kasidy Yates. You seem a bit more relaxed when you're with her. And you really do need to relax more."

Sisko frowned, still eyeing his monitors.

"Have I mentioned our wedding-day special?"

Quark asked. "All the food and liquid refreshment your guests can pack away, continuous entertainment imported from the farthest reaches of the galaxy, and all for a price even a Bimenion could afford?"

"If the Bimenion's as rich as Croesus," Sisko mumbled.

The Ferengi turned back to the helm controls. "I do believe I detect a note of sarcasm. But that's all right. Just because I'm giving you a deal I wouldn't give to my own brother—"

"Damn!" Sisko cried.

Even before he whirled in his seat, Quark knew he wasn't going to like what came next. "What is it?" he inquired.

Sisko shot an angry look at him. "We're being pursued by a pack of Orion raiders. Looks like your friend Calculanthra had second thoughts about letting us leave."

The Ferengi was out of his chair like a shot. Skidding to a halt at Sisko's side, he peered over the captain's shoulder at his monitor array.

Sure enough, the tactical screen showed him a formation of four small ships. And from what he knew of Orion technology, they were every bit as fast as the *Defiant*.

"You're right," he said. "The scoundrels! I should never have trusted that slimy Orion!"

"Too late for that now," Sisko told him.

"Activate the cloak," Quark advised. "Quickly!"

"Just what I was thinking," said his companion.

But before either of them could move, the Ferengi

felt the deck lurch beneath his feet—once, twice, and then again. Groping wildly, he caught the edge of Sisko's chair and hung on for dear life.

Wrestling himself to his feet, he asked, "What was that?"

Sisko's frown was deeper than before. "They must have gotten their hands on a Romulan vessel or two," he noted, "because they knew just where to hit us. Our cloaking capability is shot to hell."

"But how did they know we could cloak?" Quark wondered.

"Apparently," Sisko said, "word gets around."

"Fantastic," the Ferengi moaned. "Then we're sunk, aren't we? I mean, there's no way we can outmaneuver so many of them."

Inexplicably, Sisko's features reorganized themselves into a smile. "I guess we'll see about that."

"What are you going to do?" Quark asked.

On the *Laslapadil*, Calculanthra grunted as he shifted his weight in the command seat. His hirelings moved here and there about the bridge, making adjustments at the raider's various tactical stations.

The viewscreen in front of him displayed the lonely figure of the human's ship as it accelerated in an effort to shake them. He laughed.

Perhaps needless to say, that effort would meet with failure. No ship in the quadrant could outrun an Orion raider—not even the Federation's Galaxy-class giants.

He had already knocked out the other ship's cloaking device with a few well-placed shots. Of course, that was before the Federation vessel could erect its tactical shields. It would be more difficult to knock out propulsion or weapons capabilities, now that its defenses were up.

But far from impossible, the Orion noted. In a matter of moments, he'd begin battering away at the vessel's engines. Nor would he stop until he'd blasted a hole in the Federation vessel's shields, exposing the ship's warp core to his fire.

And after that, he mused, he would erase the shame of his defeat by erasing the human and his companion from existence. They should have known better than to trust to his goodwill after making him lose face with his clan and his customers.

Unfortunately, killing them would not make anyone forget the incident. But it would ease his pain to know his antagonists were in worse shape than he was.

"Faster!" he bellowed, pounding on his armrest for effect.

His hirelings did their best to squeeze a bit more speed out of the raider, though it cost them power that would normally have gone to their shields.

Satisfied, Calculanthra nodded. It wouldn't be long now.

Suddenly the Federation vessel plummeted off their screen. As the *Laslapadil*'s sensors made an adjustment to keep track of it, the Orion found himself looking at its underbelly instead of the photon spill from its warp nacelles.

"What's going on?" he roared.

One of Calculanthra's hirelings turned to him, surprise and trepidation mingled in his expression. "They're coming at us from below!" he yelled back.

Calculanthra cursed at the top of his lungs. He hadn't expected that his prey would double back on him. After all, most starships couldn't execute so tight an arc. Hell, they couldn't even come close.

But *this* one had.

"What are you doing?" Quark cried, clinging to the back of Sisko's seat.

"Teaching the Orions a lesson," the human replied. "Namely, that superior numbers are just *one* way to achieve a tactical advantage."

The Ferengi peered at the *Defiant*'s main view-screen, where he saw the undersides of the Orion raiders looming closer and closer at an alarming rate of speed. Just as it looked as if they were going to plow into one, it sheared off—and nearly speared another one in its confusion.

Blanching, he turned to Sisko. "You want to get us *killed?*" he squealed.

The captain shot him a look. "I think you're confusing me with those other guys," he said. "The ones who are trying to blow us out of existence."

Setting his teeth, Quark watched as Sisko's fingers flew across his controls. Apparently he'd slaved all the ship's functions to this one location. And it was a good thing he had, considering how useless the Ferengi himself would have been in this situation.

Abruptly the viewscreen went ruby-red with several short devastating bursts of phaser fire. When the screen cleared, Quark could see that one of the Orions had been disabled, a huge gash in one of its flanks. But he only got a glimpse of it, because Captain Sisko was executing yet another dizzying maneuver.

One of the raiders shot toward them, looking for all the world as if it would hit them head-on—but they veered off at the last moment. There was a second prolonged display of lurid light, but the Ferengi couldn't tell if it found its target.

"Did we get him?" he asked.

The captain nodded. "We got him. Two down, two to go."

"Unless they just give up," Quark suggested hopefully.

"They won't," Sisko informed him, still very much intent on his controls. "They're Orions, remember? They don't know *how* to give up."

The words were barely out of his mouth when the deck leaped again beneath the Ferengi's feet. This time, he couldn't hang on to Sisko's chair. He lost his footing, went rolling head over heels. And by the time he stopped, he was lodged under the overhang of a perimeter station.

Strangely, however, his first thought wasn't for himself. It was for the human in command. Crawling out from under the perimeter station, he saw that Sisko had been thrown halfway out of the center seat.

And he was in pain. *Great* pain. His features were

clenched like a fist, and there were traces of fresh blood around the rent in his uniform.

"Oh my," Quark said, frightened to find out how badly their ship had been damaged. "Oh my," he said again.

By the time he worked up the courage to approach the human, Sisko was already climbing back into his seat to survey the situation. A moment later, he eyed his control console. The Ferengi couldn't tell if it was the captain's pain or their prospects that made the man grimace like that.

"Did they incapacitate us?" he asked meekly, dreading the answer.

But it was better than he'd feared. Much better.

"We're all right," Sisko told him. "Just a few circuits off-line." He looked up at Quark. "The helm's no longer slaved to my control console, though." He licked his lips. "I need your help," he whispered.

The Ferengi recoiled. *"My* help? But—what can *I* do? *You're* the one with the combat experience."

The captain shook his head. "I can't be in two places at once," he insisted. "And you've never fired a phaser out in space. You're going to have to man the helm."

Quark was about to protest some more, but something on the viewscreen caught his eye. Looking back over his shoulder, he saw that the two unscathed Orion ships were wheeling for a pass at them.

"All right," he said. "All right, already." Scampering for the helm station, he inserted himself behind the controls. "I'm here," he announced. "What do I do?"

"Head right for them," Sisko said. "Full impulse."

The Ferengi couldn't help seeing their death in that strategy—but there was no time to argue about it. He would just have to hope the captain's brains hadn't been scrambled in that last skirmish.

Biting his lip, he carried out the order. Unfortunately, the Orions seemed to have the same idea. Their ships grew bigger and bigger as they approached, until Quark wanted to dive for cover.

Then, when it seemed that a collision was unavoidable, the enemy lost his nerve. Both ships peeled away—and it proved their undoing.

The Ferengi saw two separate barrages of red phaser energy reach out and stab the Orions. Both, he knew right away, were knockout blows.

A moment later, the screen shifted to a rear view— and Quark was pleased to see his observation was right on the money. Their last two adversaries were coasting awkwardly, without photon trails. Somehow, Sisko had found their weak spots and exploited them simultaneously.

Quark turned to him. "Nice shooting."

"Thanks," Sisko said. With an effort, he got up and headed aft—no doubt, in search of a medkit. "Just do one more thing for me, will you?"

"What's that?" asked the Ferengi.

The captain winced. "Take us home."

CHAPTER

13

HALKARM HAD BEEN in Manimoujak's employ for a number of years. His assignment was a simple one—he did what Manimoujak told him to do, when he was told to do it. And he didn't stop doing it until he was finished.

If Manimoujak, for example, told him to club someone to death, Halkarm would pummel away until the victim stopped moving. It was no more involved than that. If Manimoujak told Halkarm to hold his breath until he passed out, Halkarm would suck in air and stand there until the world turned black around him and he crashed to the ground.

In this case, Manimoujak had told him one thing: guard the mountain pass and make sure no one got through. And that particularly applied to those damnable Bajoran women.

This, Halkarm was more than prepared to do. His blaster rifle was tucked securely under his arm, ready to be brought into play at a moment's notice.

He wasn't the only guard on duty, of course. Others studded strategic points along the way. But Halkarm considered himself the best and most single-minded, which—to be fair—he was.

He stood on the edge of a particularly narrow ledge. He had a clear view overlooking the path in front of him. To his back, there was a sheer drop. It was a good position to maintain, because he was unassailable from all sides except above, and above simply wasn't a possibility.

In order to get at him from that direction, one would have to climb up and over, scaling some incredibly treacherous terrain, then cling batlike to the side of the mountain with a deathly drop below. No, it was most definitely not a possibility.

All this went through Halkarm's mind, up until the moment he felt a trickle of pebbles falling down from overhead. He looked up just in time to see a pair of booted feet descending toward him at high speed.

Kira slammed into the giant of a guard, knocking him back and sending his blaster rifle clattering to the side. It did not, however, fall off the perch; it just skittered to the edge.

She scrambled to her feet on the narrow ledge just in time to face Halkarm. He came at her with a roar that seemed to shake the mountain around them.

"You shouldn't have come back!" he howled at her, and at the moment, Kira was hard-pressed to disagree.

Fortunately she was quicker than the guard. As he reached for her, she sidestepped his rush and kicked him square in the ribs. But her adversary didn't seem to register the impact. Instead he grabbed her by the upper arm with a grip that made a vise seem like a love squeeze.

Kira tried to kick him in the groin, but somehow missed by a significant couple of inches. Then he got a hold of her other arm as well. Lifting her above his head, he staggered over toward the brink of the cliff so he could pitch her off.

The major slammed a foot into the guard's face. He grunted but didn't drop her. She kicked a second and a third time, and finally he stumbled, releasing her.

But he had released her over the brink.

As Kira fell, she twisted in midair. Somehow, her desperate fingers caught the edge of the cliff. Her body swung down and slammed against it, and she gasped from the impact. Above her, the guard's nose was bleeding. He wiped the blood away as he stared down at the dangling woman.

Then he smiled savagely and brought his foot up—with the obvious intention of tromping down on her fingers, which would send her plummeting to her death.

"Next time you want to fight Halkarm," he said, "you better bring plenty of friends."

And then a rock the size of a fist hurtled down from

above, smashing him just below the base of his skull. He staggered forward and tripped over one of Kira Nerys's wrists.

For a moment, the guard's arms pinwheeled, as if trying to grab a hold of the air itself. Whatever he thought he would accomplish, he wasn't successful. With a howl of indignation, he pitched forward.

Kira plastered herself against the cliffside as Halkarm tumbled over her and plummeted with a roar toward the base of the mountain. He struck the side a couple of times as he fell, then hit the ground with a sickening thud.

The major looked up as Ro and Varis descended to the outcropping from which she was dangling. Ro had a disruptor strapped to her belt.

"You certainly took your sweet time," Kira said, starting to reach up for Ro.

And then the rock crumbled beneath her, and Kira started to slip off. Ro's hand lashed out with lightning speed, snagging the major by the wrist just in time.

Kira's full weight was now being supported by the Maquis. For a fleeting second, her eyes met Ro's, and she saw the determination there. Her companion wasn't going to let her go—not for anything. Not even if the two of them tumbled to their deaths.

"Varis!" shouted the Maquis, and the tetrarch was immediately at her side, grabbing Kira's other wrist. The major tried to find purchase with the toes of her boots, but there was none. She was entirely dependent on her comrades as they pulled her to safety.

Once back on solid ground, Kira lay on her back for some moments, gasping. Then she pulled herself together and eyed Ro and Varis.

"Thank you," she said. "That was . . . appreciated." She glanced at the disruptor on Ro's belt. "Where did you get that?"

"Off the guard about twenty meters away. I didn't think he'd be needing it anymore."

Kira smiled grimly. "I'll say this for you, Ro. You may be obnoxious, but you're damned efficient."

"Thank you," said the Maquis. "Those are my two best qualities. Now . . . I think you said something about hidden entrances?"

"What do you mean, you can't raise them?" Manimoujak said angrily. He paced his monitor room. "Try again!"

Zeber tapped the comm controls for the umpteenth time. "Posts three, seven, and eight, report in!" He looked up at Manimoujak helplessly. "Still nothing, sir."

"Get posts one and two to find out what happened to the others!" Manimoujak railed. He continued to pace as Zeber endeavored to contact the other two posts. When he looked back at Manimoujak, it was not with a particularly happy expression.

"They're not answering, either."

Manimoujak couldn't quite believe what he'd just heard. "They were there a minute ago! Is the entire communications system crashing?"

"The comm system is fine, sir."

"Then what the hell is going on?!"

"I'll tell you!" came an angry pained voice. Manimoujak turned, saw who was speaking, and shrieked in alarm.

When the wall slid aside, Kira was the first one in. She looked right and left, and saw that the narrow corridor was clear. Then, waggling her finger behind her, she signaled for Ro and Varis to follow. All three of them moved silently, on the balls of their feet, poised and ready for anything.

There was a cross corridor up ahead, and they flattened against the wall. Kira poked her head around tentatively. Nothing. She started to move, Ro directly behind her, Varis bringing up the rear.

That's when Kira saw the knife out of the corner of her eye.

It was pinwheeling through the air, coming from farther down the passage that lay to their right. And it was heading straight at Ro.

In Kira's mind, the moment seemed to stretch out into infinity. Ro had not yet seen the knife, and she wasn't going to—at least, not in time. To the major, that was an utter certainty.

Kira lunged even as she shouted a warning, pushing Ro out of the way. Then she screeched as the knife buried itself in the fleshy part of her forearm. She went down, clutching at it and cursing inarticulately.

Varis gasped. Kira looked up and saw that the tetrarch was gazing down the corridor—in the direction from which the knife had come.

"Gnome!" Varis cried.

The major recognized the name. He was the one who had given the tetrarch the bad replicator supplies—the one who had aided in Varis's enslavement.

Gnome was charging toward them, a sneer on his lips and a phaser in his hand. He could have picked them off with the phaser, but he didn't. Kira sensed that he was after something else—vengeance maybe, judging by his sadistic expression.

He might have gotten what he wanted, too—except Ro yanked out her disruptor with a quickness that had to be seen to be believed and fired before Gnome could get off a shot.

The blast struck Gnome's hand, shattering the bones in it and knocking the weapon from his grasp. He went down shrieking and clutching at his ruined hand. Ro pounced on him, reversed the disruptor, and brought the butt down on the back of his head. The impact knocked him out cold.

Then she went back to Kira, who was lying there holding her arm. There was still a knife buried in it.

Through gritted teeth, the major said, "You're . . . quite a marksman."

"Not really," the Maquis replied. "I was aiming for his chest." She inspected the wound. "God, look at you. Next time, just shout a warning, okay?"

"Wasn't time," Kira told her. "Besides . . . now we're even . . . for your saving me on the cliffside."

Ro appeared to consider the notion. "Well, actually, since I nailed Gnome, that puts me one ahead."

Kira looked at her through eyes narrowed with pain. "Do you have any idea how annoying you are?"

"I've been informed of that, yes," Ro said. "And this is going to be even more annoying. Here, bite down on this." She shoved the gun butt between Kira's teeth. Then the Maquis looked up at Varis and said, "Hold her down."

As Varis moved around to Kira's uninjured shoulder and braced her, Ro tore a length of cloth off her shirt sleeve. Ro waited until Varis was in position, then looked down at Kira. The major nodded.

"By the way . . . thanks," Ro muttered, and then she slid the knife out of Kira's arm.

Kira's back arched as she sunk her teeth into the unyielding gun butt of the disruptor. Ro quickly tied off the wound. The cloth became blood-soaked in a matter of seconds, but it finally stanched the flow.

"Can you flex your fingers?" asked the Maquis.

Kira tentatively did so and then repeated the action with more confidence.

"I don't think it did any serious muscle damage," Ro said. "You were lucky."

"You have a very broad definition of luck," the major replied sarcastically. She sat up, stretching the arm. "I've had enough of this," she growled. "Let's go find our host and settle accounts."

Her companions helped her to her feet and they took off down the corridor. Kira wobbled only once as she fought off a slight wave of dizziness. Mainly, she was all right.

It was an indication of Manimoujak's supreme

confidence—some would say overconfidence—that he had not tried to move his base of operations after Kira, Ro, and Varis had broken out of the Place. Clearly, he had been certain that he was invulnerable in his lair. He had not counted on Kira's thorough knowledge of the mountains, or their collective determination to both complete their mission and pay him back for what he had done to them.

The women encountered several more guards along the way, but luck remained with them. They always managed to get the drop on them, and between Ro's consistently bad—but mysteriously effective—aim, and Kira's overall bad mood, they managed to make short work of them. Varis stayed back and watched her comrades with a mixture of awe and terror.

Then they turned a corner and suddenly there was Manimoujak, leaning over the shoulder of one of his lieutenants who was, in turn, leaning over a communications system.

"Then what the hell is going on?" Manimoujak was demanding.

Making no attempt to choke back her fury, Kira said, "I'll tell you!"

Manimoujak spun and faced them with alarm. "Wh—What—?" he stammered, and started to run.

Kira practically vaulted the distance between them. Manimoujak had retreated no more than a few steps when the major took him down, her knees landing in the small of his back.

His lieutenant was on his feet, but he obviously

wasn't a fighter. This became evident when Ro knocked him flat with one punch.

Kira pressed the business end of a knife against the underside of Manimoujak's throat.

"Now . . . now listen to me," he croaked.

"No," Kira snapped, "you listen to me. Let me explain your problem here. You didn't take us seriously. You've gotten so used to thinking of women as hunks of meat to be bartered and traded, you didn't think we posed any sort of threat. Laren, would you say we're pretty threatening?"

Ro nodded. "Yeah, Nerys, I'd say so. Sul?"

Varis nodded, too.

Kira pressed the knife against Manimoujak's flesh a little harder. "You're going to tell us what we want to know," she advised him. "You're going to tell us *everything* we want to know. Got that? Otherwise, by the Prophets, you'll have an ear-to-ear smile that's not on your face."

Manimoujak's eyes opened wide. "You . . . you wouldn't . . ."

"Actually," Ro said, "I think she would. And you have to remember something—she's the level-headed one. I'm the criminal type. So in case you were planning to appeal to me for mercy, you can pretty much forget that."

"You . . . won't do anything to me," the Yridian said, clearly trying to build up his confidence. "Not as long as you think I'll tell you what you want to know . . ."

And then he yelped as the knife dug deeper into his

skin. A trickle of blood made its way down the side of his throat.

"I'm just trying to save time," Kira hissed. "If we have to kill you and then check your computer records to find what we need, then that's what we'll do. You've got until the count of three to talk, and then I'm done with you and you're done with this life. And you can explain your actions to whatever gods the Yridians answer to. One . . . two . . . thr—"

"All right!" Manimoujak rasped. "I'll tell you!"

And he did. He described the entire distribution network through which the replicators and their virus-laden raw material had arrived on Bajor.

The Orions were the ones who had procured the stuff. Through a series of Yridian middle men, they had gotten it to Manimoujak. And Manimoujak had gotten it to Gnome.

"Everything obtained through layers upon layers," Kira noted.

"Yes," Manimoujak confirmed. "But everyone benefited, don't you see? Do you have any idea how many lives were improved, how many lives were saved, through our activities? Perhaps we profiteered a bit, but show me the merchant who operates at a loss. There were no victims—"

"No victims?" Kira resisted the impulse to press her blade a little deeper into his flesh. "You were ready to sell us on the auction block! How can you say there were no victims?"

The Yridian groaned softly. "We sold off trouble-makers, dissidents, the dregs of the Bajoran populace.

The ones no one in authority wanted around anymore. Do you seriously think we could have continued our operations if someone in the government hadn't turned a blind eye to it all? Documents had to be signed, investigations squelched . . ."

The enormity of what he was saying slowly began to sink in on Kira. She turned to Ro as if looking for confirmation of it. The Maquis nodded.

"What you're telling us," Ro said slowly, "is that anyone who had opinions contrary to the government might be branded as a troublemaker . . . and just disappear one night into the Orion slave system?"

Manimoujak nodded.

"I don't believe it," Kira whispered. "I don't believe it."

"It certainly explains why those old cronies of yours were happy to play along with the system," Ro observed. "People who might actually have been of help to us . . . were already long gone."

"It was a mutually useful system," Manimoujak said. "And it would have kept on going perfectly fine . . . a nice little under-the-table situation . . . if it hadn't been for this disease."

Varis Sul stepped forward. "Was it intentional?" she demanded.

"I don't think so," the Yridian told her. "Certainly not on my end, I can tell you that. Bajor is my base of operations. It's an old saying for those in my line of work that you don't befoul your own sandbox. If I'd known, I'd never have let it go through. So if it was a plan, it originated outside of my circle."

"And the government official," Varis said. "The one who you said was helping matters along . . ."

"I don't know," Manimoujak grated.

"Oh, come on!" Kira urged. "You expect us to believe that?"

"I don't!" he pleaded. "All I ever knew was a code name—Black Hole. How's that for melodrama? One of my men acted as a go-between. He was the only one who ever saw Black Hole in person."

"Which of your men?" Ro demanded.

The Yridian swallowed. "Halkarm."

Kira exchanged looks with the Maquis.

"That guard who fell to his death," Ro said. "Didn't I hear him say his name was—?"

Kira nodded. "Halkarm."

She slid off Manimoujak and sat glaring at him. "I don't care what kind of face you try to put on it," she said to him tightly. "You made your money from other people's misery. You're slime."

With an effort, the Yridian got to his feet. "I'll try not to be too hurt by your criticism," he replied.

Kira looked around the control room. She stopped when she noticed the comm equipment.

"Ro," she said, "do you think you can raise *Deep Space Nine* using that?"

"Not a problem," her comrade told her.

Moments later, the major was staring at the concerned face of her friend Dax. "My God, Kira, you look like you've been through a war."

"Only a small one," the major assured her. "Any luck with a—?"

"A cure?" The Trill shook her head. "We're still working on it."

Refusing to dwell on that news, Kira laid out, in broad strokes, what they'd been through and what they'd learned. "Unfortunately," she said in conclusion, "we still don't know the name of the Bajoran official who was directly involved in all this."

And then Odo stepped into view. "Actually . . . we do," he said. "Quark managed to obtain the information from a rather unsavory individual named Calculanthra."

"Quark did that?" Kira said skeptically. "How?"

"Gamesmanship," Odo explained—though it wasn't really much of an explanation at all. "The man's name is Ompar Tenzil. He operates out of the capital city."

Ompar Tenzil . . .

"You know him?" Ro asked Kira.

But it was Varis Sul who answered her. "I do. He's the main liaison between the government and the religious caste. He has a fairly impressive reputation."

"It'll be even more impressive when we're done with him," Kira vowed. "Dax, you've got the coordinates of this place. Send a runabout down with a security team to round up these . . . gentlemen . . . and have them placed in isolation. And since we're feeling a bit winded, we would appreciate a lift to the capital city. We and Ompar Tenzil are going to have a little . . . chat."

CHAPTER
14

O'BRIEN STOOD AT his usual place in Ops and tried for the third time to get through to Keiko's expedition. The communications situation on Bajor was worse than ever, but he had to talk to his wife. He had to find out what was going on down there.

Abruptly he got a response. It was one of the Bajorans—though not anyone he recognized.

"This is Chief O'Brien on *Deep Space Nine,*" he explained. "I need to speak with my—"

Before he could complete the sentence, the Bajoran vanished from the screen. And a moment later, Keiko appeared in his place.

"Oh, Miles!" she said.

She looked ragged and worried. O'Brien swallowed back his dismay.

"Is everything all right?" he asked, fearing the worst.

Keiko shook her head from side to side, a tear running down her cheek. And by that, even before she could say it, he knew.

Molly had the Wrath.

"Is there a cure yet?" his wife asked hopefully.

"No," O'Brien told her, his voice little more than a rasp, hollowed out with pain for his little girl. "There's nothing. But Julian is working on it." He licked his lips. "How is she?"

Keiko shrugged and brushed away a strand of hair that had fallen across her face. "She's sleeping. As far as she knows, she's just under the weather."

"But she's been diagnosed?" he pressed.

His wife nodded. "Just this morning. I tried to get through to you, but . . ." She shrugged again.

O'Brien took a deep breath, let it out. He felt scoured out, entirely without strength, without a clue as to what to say.

"Miles?"

"I'm here," he replied.

"How are things on the station?"

The chief wished he could have given her a happier answer. But he had to tell her the truth, no matter what.

"That's why I called," he said. "Morn came down with the Wrath a little while ago." He paused. "What about you, hon? How are you holding up?"

"I'm tired," she confessed. "And scared. But I'm managing."

"Of course you are," O'Brien told her. "You've always been the strongest among the three of us."

Keiko chuckled sadly. "You've never tried to get Molly to eat fresh kevas," she told him. "You should see who's stronger then."

Her smile looked crooked and ill-fitting. The chief missed her more at that moment than at any time he could remember.

"Keiko," he told her gently, "we'll get through this. Somehow."

"I hope so," she replied.

She turned, as if distracted by something off-screen. When she turned back to him, it was with a sense of urgency.

"We need to clear the channel, Miles. I . . . love you." Then the screen went dark.

O'Brien cursed beneath his breath. He felt so helpless . . . so terribly, terribly helpless. He wanted to help his wife and daughter, to be the savior they desperately needed.

But what could he do? He wasn't a physician. He couldn't find a cure for the Wrath. He sighed deeply. Maybe no one could, not even Julian.

And if that was the case, he told himself—if they were all going to die, and it was just a matter of when—he wanted to be with his family at the end. The more he thought about it, the more that seemed like the best course of action.

Certainly, he had his duty to perform, and he took it as seriously as anyone. But even duty paled beside his devotion to his wife and daughter.

Turning to Hagen, who was standing at the next console, he said, "Keep an eye on things, all right?"

The other man looked at him. "Er . . . sure, Chief."

Hagen didn't ask him where he was going. After all, O'Brien was his superior officer. But the man seemed to have a sense that something was amiss—that O'Brien wasn't just taking a moment to check some circuit junction somewhere.

Setting his jaw, the chief headed for Sisko's office, which Dax had lately commandeered. He could see her sitting inside, elbows on the desktop, holding her face between her hands. That expression was back, too—the one that told him she was a million light-years away.

O'Brien hated to leave her in such a state—in fact, he hated to leave the station in the care of someone who clearly wasn't up to it at the moment. But he'd made his decision, and he would stick to it.

As he approached, the doors to the office opened for him. Disturbed from her reverie, the Trill looked up.

"What is it?" she asked him, as if emerging from a short and unsatisfying sleep. He could see the strain on her face, in her eyes.

The chief cleared his throat. "I need an immediate leave of absence," he told her.

Dax eyed him, no doubt searching his face for a clue. "I see," she said. "May I ask why?"

He screwed up his resolve. "I'm needed on Bajor."

Dax seemed surprised by his answer. "Did Kira send for you?" she asked.

He shook his head. "No. Keiko needs me. Molly's come down with the Wrath."

The Trill swallowed. She seemed to search for words, but none came.

"You have to understand," he said, "this isn't easy for me. I've never walked away from an assignment in my life. But this is different. According to Julian, we're no closer to a cure than we were before. And if Molly's going to—to—"

He couldn't say it. He couldn't say the words.

"If that's going to happen," he went on, "I want to be there. I *need* to be there."

Dax looked away from him. She seemed to be struggling with something—struggling just as much as he was.

"You can't know what this is like," he rasped, his voice losing its strength in the face of his misery. "You can't imagine what it's like to love someone the way I love Molly, and to think that she might—"

Suddenly Dax turned to him, her eyes wide, her mouth agape. She seemed to be looking not at him, but through him. And before he could ask her what was going on, she screamed.

It was a single word. The word was *no,* and she screamed it long and loud from the depths of her heart, until the office echoed with it.

For a moment, O'Brien didn't know what to do. The Trill had always been so sane, so rational. To hear her start to shriek that way and without warning . . . it just didn't seem possible.

Then, as he was still pondering, still off-balance, Dax stopped and looked away from him. But he could still see part of her face. There was an expression on it that he had never seen there before—an expression of anguish, of horror and pain.

He came around the captain's desk and knelt before her. "Dax?" he said gently. "Are you all right?"

"My baby," she muttered. "My little girl." The Trill turned to him. "She was my little girl."

"*Your* little girl?" he said, reaching for understanding. What was she talking about? Molly was *his* daughter.

"Milayn," she whispered softly—and a bit sadly, he thought. And then a second time: "Milayn."

"Dax?" he repeated. "What's wrong?"

Then came the strangest and most unexpected thing of all. Abruptly the look in Dax's eyes changed again. Whereas a moment ago, she'd been lost in some private torment, she seemed now to be in control—perhaps more so than at any time since the captain's departure.

"Chief," she said, her voice strong and steady, "I know this disease."

Dax took a deep breath and leaned back in her chair. Across the table from her, both Bashir and O'Brien were waiting patiently for her to explain herself. The ward room was silent, except for the subtle hum of the station's power generators.

"It was about three hundred years ago," she began. "Lela—"

"One of your earlier hosts," the doctor interjected.

"Lela was my *first* host," she said. "She was a legislator, one of the first women to be named to the Trill Council. Later in her career, she was invited to a world called Andevian Two, to spend a year teaching. In those days, of course, the Trill didn't have warp-speed travel, so Lela couldn't go back and forth to visit her family. She ended up taking them along with her.

"At first, everything went well. The children liked Andevian Two. So did Lela's husband, Nareeya. They were treated well by the Andevians, who valued what Lela had to teach them. And in contrast to her experiences on Trill, Lela had lots of free time—which she spent with her family." She paused, remembering. "They were happy.

"Then a disease broke out on one of the smaller continents—a disease that seemed to defy the conventional cures. No one thought that much of it at the time, but as a representative of a learned culture, Lela was asked to visit the site of the outbreak. What's more, she *wanted* to go. She was curious. She wanted to see this disease close up, with her own eyes.

"Unfortunately, she'd hardly arrived when the disease began to pop up in other population centers. Before anyone knew it, it was all over Andevian Two—and no one was able to stop it. People began dying—by the hundreds, by the thousands—and all the Andevians could do was watch.

"Before long, Lela realized she was in over her head. She tried to rejoin her family, but transportation was at a standstill. Then word reached her that her eldest daughter had the disease."

Dax swallowed—with difficulty. But she had already steeled herself for this. She went on.

"The girl's name was Milayn. She was twelve . . . tall, dark, beautiful. She had wanted to be a legislator, like her mother. But the disease—"

Despite her preparation, Dax felt her words catch in her throat. She saw O'Brien staring at her from across the table and knew he sympathized. Bashir leaned forward.

"Take your time," he said.

But she wouldn't do that. She couldn't—not with people dying on Bajor.

"She died," said the Trill, "before Lela could get back to see her. I—" She stopped herself and started again, separating herself as much as she could from the experience. "*She* was devastated. And she couldn't draw any comfort from her symbiont. After all, Dax had never seen a host lose a member of his or her family."

The doctor frowned. "But Lela herself survived, didn't she? Or else the symbiont would have died with her."

Dax nodded. "Lela survived. So did the Andevians—but not until hundreds of thousands had succumbed. They finally came up with a treatment using local herbs and minerals."

"Herbs and minerals," O'Brien repeated wonderingly.

"And this isn't in our database?" Bashir asked.

The Trill shook her head. "Shortly after the cure was obtained, there was an upheaval in the Andevian government. The new regime blamed Lela for bringing the plague to Andevian Two. She was sent home, along with Milayn's body and the surviving members of her family. And from then on, the planet was closed to outsiders. That's why Andevian Two isn't in our database—because we haven't had contact with them in three centuries or more."

"But Lela knew what went into the cure," O'Brien said hopefully. "She did, didn't she?"

Dax nodded again. "Yes. She knew. And now that the memories are coming back, so do I."

Bashir cursed beneath his breath. "That's the breakthrough we needed," he told the Trill. "I may not have any data on Andevian biochemistry . . . but if a Trill was able to catch the disease, it can't be too different from yours, Jadzia. Or mine."

Dax turned to O'Brien. "Or Molly's," she added. "I'm just sorry I didn't think of this before. It's just that Lela was so miserable after Milayn's death, she blocked it out. So when the symbiont passed to me, the memory was buried deep in its consciousness."

She sighed. "Ever since this plague came about, Lela's experience had been lurking beneath the surface, distracting me from my duties. But it wasn't until the chief mentioned the possibility of his daughter dying that it all came flooding—came flooding—"

Abruptly, she felt a wetness on her face. Touching

her fingertips to her cheek, she realized she was crying. Setting her jaw, she willed herself to stop, but Lela's emotions were too strong—her pain too great.

"Jadzia," said the doctor, getting up and coming around the table to put a hand on her shoulder. "It's all right. You did your best."

"Julian?" O'Brien said impatiently. "If there's a chance we can beat this thing . . ."

"The chief's right," Dax agreed. "Come on. Let's go to the infirmary. We can input Lela's information there and see what we come up with."

She got up and headed for the door. But before she could get halfway, she felt a hand on her arm. It was O'Brien's.

"Thank you," he told her. "I know it couldn't have been easy for you to dredge all that up. I know how much it must have hurt."

The Trill managed something like a smile. "Thank me after we've come up with a cure," she said.

Before he could reply, she led the way to the infirmary.

At his post in Ops, O'Brien had lost count of which cup of coffee he was drinking. Upon reflection he realized that he might have been better off opting for Tarkalean tea instead. He couldn't recall the last time he had felt so anxious.

Normally he would have balked at having to deal with all the malcontented captains vying for his attention, all of them complaining about the quarantine. But he knew that Dax's help was needed in the infirmary, so he stuck it out.

"Odo to Ops."

O'Brien tapped his communicator badge. "O'Brien here. What can I do for you, Odo?"

"I called to let you know that we're exceeding our capacity, Chief. The brig is full and we're bringing in additional lawbreakers all the time."

O'Brien grunted. He sympathized with the lawbreakers, in this case. Bad enough to learn you'd been exposed to the plague in the first place—to be told you couldn't leave was even worse.

"I was just wondering," Odo said, "if I should prepare alternative accommodations."

"Couldn't hurt," he replied. "Use Cargo Bay Seven; that should suit our needs for the time being. I'll assign a team to help rig up security shielding."

"Thank you," said the shapeshifter. "Odo out."

O'Brien glanced at his monitors. For the last few hours, since Dax and the doctor had sequestered themselves in the infirmary, there had been no sign of a power spike. It was as if the station was behaving itself, knowing how much else was going wrong—and how much was likely to.

According to Bashir, Morn was just the precursor of a whole wave of victims. The fact that they hadn't materialized yet didn't mean they weren't going to. It was just a matter of time.

And when it came, it would be devastating. Just as devastating as it was on the surface, maybe.

O'Brien looked around Ops. The place was relatively quiet. The calm before the storm, he mused. The quiet before the—

Suddenly his controls began to beep at him. It only took a glance to find out why.

There was something wrong with section four-alpha of the gravity generator network. As he watched, cursing beneath his breath, generators went down one after the other.

Four-beta. Four-gamma and delta.

All of them governed personnel quarters on the habitat ring—but it was only a matter of time before the problem spread to an operations area.

The failure rate was eight percent and climbing before O'Brien could go into action. He was halfway to the turbolift when Hagen called after him.

"Chief! What's going on?"

O'Brien scowled. "It's the gravity generators! See what you can do to bleed inertia from the system until I can figure out what's gone wrong! And, for godsakes, get a team down to level seven, section five—I may need help down there!"

Hagen looked at him. "Why there?"

"Trust me," the chief told him. And without another word, he grabbed a tricorder and made his way to the turbolift.

Why level seven, section five? he echoed inwardly. Because there was a major gravity node there, located not far from the lift. And based on the pattern of generator failure, that seemed a likely problem spot.

Not that anyone on the station but O'Brien would

have known that without delving into the engineering logs. After all, it was he who'd revamped the gravity net, generator by generator, not more than a couple of years ago.

No one knew that net the way he did. Hell, no one knew the whole station the way he did.

As the lift doors opened for him, the chief stepped inside and gave it its marching orders. A moment later, he was descending into the bowels of the station, where there was still as much evidence of Cardassian technology as of the Federation variety.

Level seven, section five, he thought, rifling through his mental files for a more complete picture of the place. As it happened, that section was one of the first O'Brien had worked on when he first came aboard *Deep Space Nine*.

It was also one of the sections that had run the smoothest over the last several months. He couldn't remember the last time he'd even had to take a look at it.

Abruptly the lift doors opened. The chief stepped out—only to be confronted with a vision of chaos.

Halfway down the corridor, where the Cardassians had located the power control room for this portion of the station, the bulkhead was a red-hot sparking mess with a hole in the middle of it.

Of course, the place was no longer a "control" room in any *real* sense of the word—not since O'Brien had switched over the power feed for the gravity node from the Cardassians' microwave technology to Federation-standard electro-plasma. Now the room was like any other power juncture—run automatically by the station computer.

As the chief approached it, tricorder out, he began to understand what had been happening to the station over the last few days. The power spikes he'd encountered over and over again, the ones he couldn't seem to find the source of . . . *this* must have been their source.

Whatever had happened inside the control room must have had repercussions throughout the EPS system, sending spikes up one conduit after the other like shock waves radiating from an explosion. Except they'd radiated unevenly, so he'd had no simple way to find their center.

But why hadn't the sensors picked any of this up? O'Brien asked himself. Why hadn't any of the diagnostics he'd run unearthed the problem?

Then he had an inkling what the answer might be. Venturing closer to the control room, he peered inside its open doorway, looking for evidence that would support his theory.

He found some. For as he stared through squinting eyes past the sparks and the unholy red glow, he could see that the internal sensor leads for this section—the ones he'd installed when he switched over the power conduits to EPS—were blackened and fused.

He wasn't sure what had happened to them. It could've been caused by any one of a number of malfunctions—in fact, he saw this type of minor damage all the time. But if his diagnostic checks hadn't picked it up, it was because something unusual had happened.

Something his tricorder confirmed. O'Brien sighed.

The sensor leads hadn't just burned out. They'd formed some kind of feedback loop, creating the false impression that they were still working. And because of that—because he'd had no hint the sensors were on the blink—he'd also had no way to know there'd been a power anomaly.

Ironically, all the problems caused by the energy spikes had been fairly far from this point. It was only now that something as close as the gravity node down the corridor had been affected—and, in turn, taken down generator after generator. Perhaps the greatest surprise of all was that the node hadn't been damaged until now.

"Chief?" came a voice.

O'Brien turned and saw the arrival of the team he'd asked for, complete with tool boxes and EM field projectors. He recognized the faces of all three of them: Orser, Eisenman, and Yamaguchi—two men and a woman. All young and relatively inexperienced, but with the basic tools they'd need to become starship engineers one day.

That is, if they survived their stint on *Deep Space Nine,* and that was always a crapshoot.

"Seems we've located the source of all those power spikes," he told them. He tilted his head to indicate the control room. "It's in there. We fix this and the gravity control problem stops spreading."

Orser nodded. "We'll set up the projectors and get started."

"You do that," the chief replied. "I'll coordinate things with Mr. Hagen at Ops." He tapped his combadge. "O'Brien here. We've pinpointed the generator problem—and the reason for the power spikes as well. What's going on up there?"

"It's not good," the younger man told him. "Gravity generators are going down right and left. I've notified security."

"Good thinking," O'Brien said. "How much time before the gravity loss spreads to a critical area?"

There was a pause. "At this rate, not long," Hagen replied at last. "Ten minutes, if we're lucky—but more likely, around seven."

"Thanks," the chief said. "Keep me posted and vice versa. O'Brien out."

By then, the engineering team was almost finished setting up its forcefield projectors—the same kind Odo was using to pen up his lawbreakers. Except O'Brien's bunch would be dealing with deadly electro-plasma, not just some ornery Benzite.

There was quite a bit to do, too. First, they would have to locate the exact point of the energy leak. Then they would have to put an electromagnetic "bandage" over it and seal it up via micro-laser.

It wouldn't be as easy as simply cutting power to this section of the station—but that would mean a sweeping loss of gravity and the inertial stresses that came with it, and that was what they were trying to avoid. Better to do it this way and minimize the danger to the rest of *Deep Space Nine*—if not to themselves.

Yamaguchi turned to O'Brien as soon as the projectors were in place. "We're ready to go in," she informed him.

"I'll do it," he insisted. "Just keep an eye on me in case something goes wrong. My delicate skin won't stand up to naked plasma for long."

Yamaguchi smiled. "We'll keep an eye on you, all right."

Fortunately, nothing *did* go wrong. O'Brien entered the control room with a couple of the instruments his assistants had brought down, manipulated one of the EM force projectors so that its field covered the leak, and then set about repairing it.

It took all of six and a half minutes to weld the conduit closed with his micro-laser. Then, sweat streaming from his forehead and drenching his tunic, he got up and went out to see his team.

"And that," he told them, "is how it's done." He tapped his communications badge again. "O'Brien to Hagen. We're finished down here."

"I can tell," said the ensign. "The generator problem has stabilized. Of course, we've still got to bring the ones that *were* affected back on-line . . ."

The chief winked at his team. "I think I've got just the personnel for that, Mr. Hagen. O'Brien out."

Orser, Eisenman, and Yamaguchi looked at him.

The chief couldn't help but notice a hint of admiration in their eyes.

"Well," he said, "what are you waiting for? There's a gravity node to repair, and all those generators to bring back on-line."

"We're on it," Eisenman assured him. And a moment later, they took off down the corridor with all their equipment.

O'Brien wiped some perspiration from his brow. All was well that ended well, he told himself. Pretty soon, everything would be back to normal.

But it could have happened differently. A *lot* differently.

If he had abandoned his post as he'd had a mind to . . . if someone else had been manning his station up in Ops . . . they wouldn't have been able to trace the generator problems to their source the way he had. It would have taken a section-by-section search.

And by then a quarter of the station might have lost gravity. People could have been hurt. Damage could have been done to other, even more crucial systems. Even the infirmary might have been affected.

The chief winced. The infirmary—where Bashir and Dax were working on the cure. He couldn't help but picture the doctor and the Trill floating in midair, their work ruined by the sudden loss of gravity.

If O'Brien hadn't known where to locate the generator problem, their ability to fight the plague might have been lost—or at least drastically delayed. And who knew how many lives might have been lost as a result?

Including one very small, very special life. The chief winced again.

But he *had* stayed, hadn't he? He had remained at his post. He had been here to ward off the impending disaster.

And that, he realized, had made all the difference.

CHAPTER 15

VARIS SUL lapsed into silence during their trip to the capital city. Kira offered to return her to the Paqu village, but she declined.

After all, she wanted to meet the author of her misery face to face.

Her downward spiral had begun with her encounter with the trader who had given her the worthless antidote. Since then, through her subsequent capture and her near-sale into slavery, through the pain and degradation she had suffered, she had been convinced she was doing some sort of penance for her actions.

She had not expected to survive it all. Sul was certain her destiny was to suffer, and continue to suffer, until she finally succumbed to the disease herself. Ostensibly, her plan was to try and find some way of saving her people, but she didn't really think she had a chance of achieving that. Not really.

Then she was liberated by Kira Nerys and Ro Laren. She watched them in action, admired their resolve, their bravery. And slowly, slowly, something had begun to stir in her. A bit of that spark, that fire . . . that desire that had enabled her to become the tetrarch in the first place.

It was that same spark that demanded she confront her tormentor. It required that she look him in the eye and tell him what he had done to her and her people.

Only then could she accept whatever fate the Prophets had in store for her.

Before long, their runabout brought them to the offices of Ompar Tenzil. They were extremely plush, located in one of the central government buildings.

Varis, Kira, and Ro provided a stark contrast to their surroundings. They were bruised and bedraggled, cut and bandaged. The runabout pilot had tried to talk them into coming back to *Deep Space Nine* to be patched up, but they would have none of it. In a way, they considered their disheveled appearance a badge of honor.

It seemed bizarre—that after everywhere they had been, all the frightening and sleazy places they had passed through, the trail should end here in such comfortable surroundings.

Ompar's personal assistant, a buxom brunette, offered them a beverage while they waited. She indicated the overstuffed couch with a gesture.

"We're not especially interested in waiting," Kira announced.

The assistant had a permanent smile affixed to her face. "You must understand, Ompar Tenzil is a busy man. If you'll take a seat, I'll see if I can squeeze you in sometime in the next—"

Ro brushed by the woman. "That's very kind, but I think we'll squeeze ourselves in." Without another word, she kicked open the door to Ompar's office.

The secretary emitted a shrill protest, but by that point, Varis and Kira had passed her as well. As the three women entered the office, they found Ompar at his desk.

There was no one with him. He wasn't in communication with anyone. He wasn't going through work that sat in front of him, or doing much of anything. His computer terminal was on, and there was something on the screen.

It was Ompar's own image. He had apparently been in the middle of recording some sort of personal journal. But now he was simply staring off into space, looking out through the sizable windows that opened onto a spectacular view of the city.

With a strange lack of urgency, he shifted his gaze and looked up at them. "Yes?"

"Ompar Tenzil?" Kira said briskly. "You've been named as a co-conspirator in a black-market scheme—"

"In the black market, yes," Ompar Tenzil said faintly. He didn't seem to care that they were accusing him of anything, or even that they were in the room.

"Yes. That's right. And there's really not much of anything you can do about it."

At that moment, Varis felt a scratching in her throat, a distant heaviness in her lungs. And she knew. It was the first, earliest sign, the most preliminary of symptoms. But she knew that finally, finally, the Wrath had caught up with her.

And that was when she snapped.

All the rage, all the hurt, all the fury that had roiled within her suddenly bubbled over. She had never seen Ompar Tenzil before, never had any dealings with him. He had not physically hurt her in any way.

But Ompar Tenzil was in the wrong place at the wrong time, and Varis's unfettered anger was unleashed at him. With a growl that sounded completely wrong in a humanoid throat, she leaped at him, her fingers outstretched.

As they wrapped themselves around his throat, she bore him backward, knocking him off the chair. The two of them tumbled to the floor.

"Get off him!" Kira shouted.

"Come on, let him go!" Ro admonished.

It took the efforts of both women to pull Varis off the man. Slowly he sat up, dusting off his bulk and not looking particularly put off by the way he'd just been handled.

"He admits it!" Varis hissed. "He admits what he did, and he doesn't care! He doesn't care!"

Ompar got to his feet, with an expression of incredible sadness. "You're right, my dear. I don't." He tapped the computer terminal. "You'll find here all the records you need to dismantle the trade links through the black market. Some of it you may already have, but I'm sure there's much that'll be of value to you."

"It's a trick!" Varis snapped.

She struggled against Ro's grip, but couldn't get anywhere. The woman was a lot stronger than she looked.

"A trick?" Ompar echoed. He seemed surprised. "No, my dear. It's no trick. Think of it as . . . a parting gift."

Kira glared at him. "You don't think we're just going to let you walk away, do you?"

The official regarded her. "Walk? Oh, no."

And then, without another word, Ompar Tenzil dashed toward the window. He moved with startling speed for one of his bulk.

Kira took a step, trying to stop him, but he was out of reach. He slammed into the glass with his shoulder and it shattered, giving way before his charge.

He was out into midair and, for a moment, seemed to hover there as if he were going to fly away over the spires of the city. Then gravity seized hold of him, and he fell.

The women ran to the window and watched helplessly as he plummeted toward the ground. He didn't scream, he didn't make a sound. His arms were outstretched as if he were a wounded bird, and when he hit the ground he was so far down they didn't hear the impact. All they heard were the screams of passersby who had witnessed the suicide.

For a long moment, Varis and her companions said nothing. They looked at each other in stunned confusion. Then, as if operating with one mind, they went to the computer and activated the program on it.

The screen showed them a suicide note from Ompar Tenzil. Ompar Tenzil, trader and traitor, black marketeer. Ompar Tenzil, who had just learned that he had the Wrath, and decided he wasn't interested in waiting for the illness to run its fatal course.

His last request was for forgiveness from the Prophets. Somewhere, Varis imagined, the Prophets were laughing at the man's arrogance.

Bashir had done it. He had discovered a cure for the virus.

Again.

Except this time, the damned thing wasn't going to mutate and ruin his moment of triumph. This time, he had beaten it once and for all.

"Well?" he said, turning to Dax. "What do you think?"

She was gazing at the monitor in front of them, which displayed a microscopic multitude of the virus helixes. They weren't bent, either, since Bashir had abandoned his original approach to dealing with them. But they were also no longer purple.

They were a silvery white. A most attractive silvery-white, now that he thought about it—and not only because of the way it looked to him. This particular silvery-white meant that the viruses had been sheathed—isolated from their environment.

In short, they had suffocated it with a mineral-based compound—a close variation on the theme invented by the Anderians centuries earlier, when it had been their turn to confront the plague.

Dax nodded. "That's it," she confirmed.

And of course, she would be the one to know. As Lela Dax, she was the only one now living who had seen the Andevians' cure.

"Of course, we still have to test it," Bashir said. "That will require a volunteer. And since we have only one full-blown case of the plague here on the station . . ." He let his voice trail off as he glanced in the direction of Morn's bio-bed.

The Trill looked at him. "Morn's not going to be a willing guinea pig."

"Perhaps not," the doctor acknowledged, as he led the way into the quarantine area. "But I think I've got a way to convince him."

Dax grunted. "The prospect of dying isn't going to do it," she noted. "Morn is one big baby when it comes to things like this."

"Actually," Bashir said, "I had a different motivation in mind. A bribe, as it were. Free drinks at Quark's—or Rom's, as it's called now—for a month."

Despite the seriousness of the situation, the Trill couldn't help but chuckle. "For that, I think he just might heal *himself.* But don't you think we should ask Rom first?"

The doctor shook his head. "We're doing him a

favor, aren't we? If everyone on the station perishes, who's going to patronize his place?"

Dax nodded. "Good point."

"I thought you'd appreciate it," Bashir replied.

Then he approached Morn with the terms of his offer.

CHAPTER
16

DEEP SPACE NINE had never looked so good to Sisko as it did now on his monitor. He turned to Quark, who was still at the helm controls.

"Don't worry," the Ferengi assured him. "I'll take care to dock your ship without damaging it. After all, I'd like to get home safely, too."

The captain grunted. "I never doubted the strength of your instinct for self-preservation."

"And my piloting skills?" Quark asked.

"As a pilot," Sisko gibed, "you make a hell of a bartender."

Tapping his communications padd, he opened a channel to Ops. "This is Captain Sisko," he said. "Requesting permission to dock."

Dax's face appeared a moment later. And she was smiling. "Welcome home, Benjamin."

The captain looked at her. "Dare I hope . . . ?" he began.

"We've found a cure," she confirmed, "one that we tested successfully. In fact, we're pumping it through the station's ventilation system right now."

"The station?" Sisko inquired.

She nodded. "After you left, it began to show up in non-Bajorans. But there haven't been any casualties."

"I see," he said. "And what about Bajor? How are you going to deliver the cure *there?*"

"Chief O'Brien suggested that we use the runabouts to seed the atmosphere. And since it was his idea— and he had a personal stake in the matter—I let him lead the mission. Also, I told him he could visit with his family when he was done. I thought he had earned that."

Of course, thought the captain. Keiko and Molly. If the plague had begun to jump species, they would be in jeopardy.

"Good idea," he agreed. "Incidentally, if this works, the Bajorans may name Bashir a Prophet."

Dax laughed softly. "Just what he needs to soothe that fragile ego of his."

Sisko laughed, too—and a pain shot through his side. He winced.

Suddenly the Trill's brow creased. "Benjamin . . . are you all right?"

"Just a few cracked ribs," he told her. "Nothing the

doctor can't handle, now that he's done saving the planet." He paused. "How's Kira?"

"Fine," Dax said, "last we heard. She's still down on Bajor, trying to find the last link in the chain of corruption—the one you and Quark supplied her with."

The captain was concerned. However, he reminded himself, Kira was a big girl. She could take care of herself. Likewise for Ro.

"We'll speak some more after we dock," he told the Trill. "Sisko—"

"Hang on a second," Quark said, leaning over so he could be seen by Dax. "How's my bar?"

The captain couldn't quite decipher the Trill's expression. But if he were the Ferengi, he knew he'd be disconcerted by it.

"I've got to go now," she replied. "Dax out."

Quark stared at the monitor for a moment. Then he harrumphed. "You know," he commented, "if I didn't know better, I'd have said she was trying to keep something from me."

Sisko looked at him, unable to resist one last jab. "Well," he said, "we'll soon find out . . . won't we?"

Keiko O'Brien stood underneath the awning in front of the Gnago Island research compound, her hair whipping savagely in the rain and the wind, and watched a massive black stormfront attack the sky like a savage beast.

Thin needles of blue-white lightning stitched the

underbelly of the dark heavy clouds. There was a distinct smell of ozone in the air, and a long vicious crack of thunder.

Keiko had needed a breath of fresh air, a brief respite from the care Molly required. And with her daughter sleeping soundly for the first time all day, she had taken the opportunity to go outside for a moment.

But only for a moment—because she couldn't forget that Molly needed her. Taking a last look at the stormfront, she went back inside and made her way through the sick ward to her daughter's bed.

Not so long ago, this room had been a research lab, dedicated to scientific study. But all the researchers were sick now, some very much so. And judging from what they'd heard over the Bajoran comm net, it was only going to get worse.

Keiko knelt by Molly's side and her daughter's eyes fluttered open—as if she knew her mother was there again. The little girl's face was flushed and feverish as she looked up at Keiko.

"Is it a big storm, Mommy?"

"A very big storm," Keiko confirmed.

The girl grunted softly. "It's a good thing we're not in the mountains anymore—right, Mommy?"

Keiko smiled down at her daughter and nodded. "You're a smart girl, Molly. If we were in the mountains in this kind of weather, we'd all have been in big trouble."

Her daughter was silent for a moment. She seemed to be thinking about something. Thinking *hard*.

"Mommy?"

"Yes, love?"

"Fola Mirax says the storm is the Prophets' way of saying they're mad at us."

Keiko frowned. It was impossible to be on Bajor and not hear such talk these days. She regretted now that she'd decided to come on this expedition—that she'd put them both in such terrible danger. She'd just never expected anything like this.

"Well," she said at last, "we're not Bajoran. We don't have to believe in the Prophets if we don't want to." It was an awkward way to say it, but at least she'd gotten her point across.

The girl sighed. "Fola Mirax says that's why they're mad. Because there are so many people from other planets on Bajor now—people who don't believe in them."

Keiko cursed Fola Mirax beneath her breath. "Don't believe everything you hear," she advised Molly. "Sometimes people say silly things when they're scared."

Molly looked up at her again. "Are you scared, Mommy?"

Damned right I am, thought Keiko. But of course, she wasn't going to admit that to her daughter. "Not really," she lied.

"Not even of the plague?" Molly pressed.

"Not even of the plague," Keiko told her, with an assurance she didn't feel. "And you know why?"

The little one shook her head. "No, why?"

"Because people like your daddy are working to help find a cure for it. That's why I'm not scared."

There was another crack of thunder. The walls of the place seemed to shake with it.

Oh, Miles, she thought, *where are you?*

Just then, a Bajoran standing by the door made a sound of surprise and pointed to something outside. Another Bajoran joined him, and then another, and before Keiko knew it there was a buzz all around the room.

"What is it?" she asked another woman, whose son and daughter had both come down with the plague.

The woman turned to her with a expression of curiosity and hope. "Something's landing on the grass in front of the compound. Some kind of ship, I think."

A ship? Landing here on Gnago Island, of all places? Suddenly Keiko's heart leaped. *Could it be . . . ?*

Molly tugged on her sleeve. "What is it, Mommy?"

Keiko looked down at her. She didn't want to get her daughter's hopes up, but she had to see for herself. As gently as she could, she bent and picked Molly up in her arms, blanket and all. Then she negotiated a course through the maze of beds to the open doorway.

What she saw made her breath catch in her throat. It was a ship, all right. A runabout—the kind that could only have come from *Deep Space Nine.* The rain was coming down harder now, sizzling over its smooth silvery hull.

Somehow she made her way to the front of the crowd that was forming outside beneath the awning. As she watched, her heart pounding in her chest so hard it hurt, the hatch of the runabout opened.

And out stepped Miles. Before the hatch could close behind him, the rain had turned the mustard color of his uniform a dark brown. It streamed through his hair and down the sides of his face, making it difficult for him to see.

But somehow, he saw *her*. He smiled at the sight of his wife and then his daughter, and with ever-increasing strides made his way across the grassy field to where they stood.

The Bajorans either recognized or guessed who he was. In any case, they parted like the Red Sea as he approached, leaving Keiko and Molly standing all alone in his path.

At first, there were no words said between them. They didn't need any. And besides, Keiko's throat had closed too much for her to speak.

She just reached out to Miles and held him close to her, and he hugged her back. And though Molly was too weak to hug much, she did her part as well.

"Daddy?" she whispered. "Are you helping to find a cure, like Mommy said?"

Miles beamed at her. "Not anymore, baby. We *found* one." He swiped at his eyes with the back of his hand, wiping aside what was mostly rain but not all rain, and added, "That's what all this water is about. We seeded the clouds with the cure."

Keiko looked up at the dark and tumultuous heavens, wanting to believe, but afraid to. "Is it true?" she whispered. She gazed at her husband again. "Is this the end of it?"

Her husband nodded, looking haggard and drawn and yet happier than she'd ever seen him. "It's over," he assured her. "We can go home."

Kira Nerys, patched up and scrubbed clean, suddenly found herself nostalgic for the likes of Manimoujak and his disruptor-brandishing guards. They were certainly preferable to a face-to-face meeting with Kai Winn.

Nonetheless, protocol demanded that Kira stop at the Kai's temple to pay her respects while on her way to the special session of the provisional government. It was a session that was going to deal with the black-market problem that had infested Bajor, and Kira was to be *Deep Space Nine*'s official representative.

Kira stopped at the entrance to the temple and cleared her throat loudly. "Kai Winn," she called. "It's—"

"Kira Nerys." The voice of the Kai seemed to float as if trickling down from heaven above. "Come in, my child, come in."

A little wary, Kira walked into Winn's inner sanctum and was startled by the expression on her host's face. The Kai looked overjoyed to see her.

"Kira, my dear," she said. "Enter. Enter, please. It is good to see you."

The major chose to stand a few feet away from the Kai, her hands clasped behind her back. "You look well, Kai Winn."

"Indeed," the Kai told her, "I am well. Then again, anyone who has been given a new lease on life would look well, don't you think?"

Kira shrugged. "I suppose."

"Our world is on the mend, child," said the Kai. She didn't seem to walk around the room so much as float. "You see before you one of the many who have recovered from the plague."

"I . . . had no idea you were ill," Kira told her. "I . . . am pleased, obviously, that you have recovered. You might like to know *Deep Space Nine* has sent personnel down to aid in the restoration of our world. Some of the more extreme cases needed additional medical attention, and there were secondary infections . . ."

"It will all be attended to," Kai Winn said confidently.

"Yes," the major agreed, "it will. Captain Sisko is overseeing the operation, and he's certain that—"

The Kai laughed softly. Kira had heard Winn laugh on a couple of previous occasions. In each instance, it had chilled her to the bone. Now, however, it actually sounded sincere and joyful. Frighteningly so, in fact.

"I wasn't referring to the Emissary," the Kai explained. "Oh, make no mistake, I'm sure his intentions are genuine and honorable. Whatever help he wishes to give us will be appreciated—of course. But it's not as if we really need him."

"It's not?" Kira asked.

"Not at all," Winn said. "Not in the face of the miracle."

"The . . . miracle?" The major felt clueless, as if she'd walked in on the middle of someone else's conversation.

The Kai crossed to her and placed her hands on Kira's shoulders. The major tried not to cringe.

"Don't you see, my child? All this time . . . we thought we were facing the Wrath of the Prophets. That they had called down upon us some hideous disease, designed to wipe us off the planet. But it was a test, Kira. It was a test, as so many of us who didn't lose faith believed. And the Prophets looked down from their palace, saw that their children were afflicted . . . and saw that we had not lost hope."

She turned away from Kira and spoke with her arms raised to the sky. "And they sent a cure to us. They saw our need, they saw our faith, and they wept with joy for our trust in them. Their tears came down from the clouds, showered upon us, and made us whole again."

It was all Kira could do not to laugh. "You've got to be kidding."

The Kai looked at her. "'Kidding'? My child, why would I jest about this great miracle?"

"It wasn't anything miraculous," Kira insisted. "It was the runabouts from *Deep Space Nine*. They seeded the clouds with the antidote, caused the rain that carried the antidote with it, and that was that. The Prophets weren't crying. There was just us—just mortals doing their jobs. I'm sorry if that's not spectacular enough for you, but, well . . . that's what happened."

Kai Winn sighed deeply. "My dear Kira . . . sometimes I think you will say or do anything in order to mock my beliefs."

"It's not a matter of mockery! It's—" The major threw up her hands in disgust. "Oh, what do I care. Believe what you want. Believe it was the Prophets' tears, if you want—that's probably what you're telling everybody already. Believe in whatever you want to believe in. Me, I know the truth—and that's all that matters."

The Kai made a gesture of acceptance. "You know your truth, child—and I know mine."

"Truth is truth," Kira maintained. She bowed slightly. "Good day to you, Kai." Then she turned and headed for the door.

"Kira."

The major stopped and frowned, her shoulders slightly hunched. "Yes?" she replied.

"Let us say, for the sake of argument, that you are correct—and that the cure was generated through the efforts of *Deep Space Nine*."

"Okay. Let's say that."

Winn considered her benignly. "Then tell me . . . would you dismiss the interpretation that the cure was discovered as a result of the will of the Prophets? Divine inspiration, perhaps? Would you allow this as, say, a possibility, Kira Nerys?"

The major considered her answer long and hard.

She thought about everything they had encountered, everything that she and her friends on *Deep Space Nine* had had to overcome.

"I suppose . . . it's possible, yes. When you put it that way, anything is possible."

The Kai nodded approvingly. "There's hope for you yet, Kira Nerys."

CHAPTER
17

THERE WAS ONE great constant in governments throughout the galaxy. When a problem presented itself, the same solution was invariably offered: the formation of a committee.

Which was why Kira and Ro found themselves seated before the black-market committee, convened as soon as the smuggling network was exposed. Kira didn't recognize any of the four individuals seated upon it, except for one—the committee's chairman, a severe-looking Bajoran woman named Keree Lawr.

Keree regarded both Kira and Ro as if they were some new form of bacteria. The two women had just finished giving a complete and detailed account of their experiences and encounters within the realm of the black market.

"This committee formally extends its thanks to you, Kira Nerys," said Keree Lawr, "for the names and locations you have provided us. You have our assurance that the matter will be fully investigated and the perpetrators appropriately dealt with."

There was a dead silence that hung there for a time, and then Kira said, "Is that it?"

Keree eyed her. "Yes. Unless you have something to add."

Sensing what Kira was about to say, Ro told her softly, "No, don't do it."

But the major didn't listen to her. "I think there should be some formal acknowledgment of Ro Laren's part in all this," Kira said, making no attempt to hide her annoyance. "Ro was by my side the entire time, endured the same hardships, took the same risks. You thank me and not her. Why is that?"

Keree Lawr stared at her as if she'd blown out several key brain cells. "You want an official recognition of a member of the Maquis from the Bajoran government?"

Ro was telling her this wasn't necessary, but Kira wasn't having any of it. "I want you to acknowledge that I would likely be dead if it weren't for her. Unless that doesn't matter to you, either."

With open disdain, Keree Lawr said, "It is comforting to know you think so highly of what matters and doesn't matter to your government, particularly considering how little you've been a part of it. You have been away from us, and your world, for extended periods of time, Kira Nerys—and as the Terrans say,

243

out of sight is out of mind. So I'll admit we have been giving very little thought to you one way or the other."

Kira bristled, about to fire back a response, but Keree steamrolled right over her. "As for Ro Laren, we repeat, she is part of the Maquis—an illegal organization. The Maquis may consider themselves to be well-intentioned, and the foodstuffs Ro Laren brought as an intermediate measure were appreciated. Ultimately, however, what good the Maquis has done is outweighed by the threat they pose to the young treaty with Cardassia."

Kira couldn't believe this. But then, maybe she should have expected it.

"It is going to be our recommendation to the full council," said Keree, "and our explicit instruction to you, Ro Laren . . . that you depart and not return until the Maquis has been disbanded and its leaders brought to account.

"You sit here now under a flag of truce extended by Captain Sisko, and we will not violate that understanding. And when the Maquis is no longer, your actions in this matter will certainly weigh heavily in your favor. But until that time, we suggest you leave Bajor immediately. And once you have left, under no circumstances should you return until—"

"I get the picture," Ro said sharply, getting to her feet.

No longer was she endeavoring to hold back Kira. Clearly, her own anger was coming to the forefront.

"Now let me paint a new picture for you," said the

Maquis. "This 'young treaty' of yours is never going to live to be an old treaty."

Keree leaned forward. "Is that a Maquis threat?"

"No," Ro told her. "It's a personal prediction, and its death is not going to have anything to do with the Maquis. You—you and your associates and this whole damned world—are being led into a trap by the Cardassians, and you're walking into it with a smile, sticking out your necks and inviting the executioner's ax.

"It might happen tomorrow, or a year from tomorrow, but sooner or later that trap is going to be sprung, and you'll be turning to the Maquis, begging for us to help you out. And you know what's the most sickening thing of all? We *will* help you out—because we believe in Bajor, even if Bajor doesn't believe in us."

"Are you through?" Keree asked.

"Yes," Ro said. "No . . . one other thing." She pointed at Kira. "I didn't like the way you spoke to her just then. As if she's somehow lesser than you because she's up on *Deep Space Nine* and you're down here. Kira Nerys is making more of a difference in Bajor's future through her work aboard that station than anything you pathetic little people are doing on Bajor.

"And by keeping her distance, Kira is able to avoid the whole moral mire that Bajor is getting sucked into. She's incorruptible, Keree. She can't be bought. She can't be bargained with. When she sinks her teeth into something, you can't shake her loose, no matter how much you try.

Ro's voice grew louder with righteous indignation. "And you have the nerve to look upon Major Kira with disdain? You should be praying to the Prophets that you can find a hundred more like her, rather than turning up your nose at the one you've got."

And then she turned on her heel and left the room. Without a word, Kira hurried off after her, leaving the black-market-committee members looking at each other in mild confusion.

The major caught up with Ro in the hallway outside. "I was about to head over to the main chamber," she said. "The rest of the council is in session, and they're going to be deciding what to do about Varis Sul. I thought I'd show up, give Sul some moral support. Captain Sisko will be there and . . ." She shrugged. "Do you want to come?"

Ro gave it a moment's thought. "No," she answered at last. "No, I think my being there, sitting in her corner, could only poison her chances. I'd best be on my way."

She started to walk again, and Kira called after her. "That's it?"

Ro turned to her. "That's what?"

"Well, it's . . ." Kira cleared her throat. "Those things you said about me—did you mean all that, or was it just to annoy those sanctimonious twits?"

Ro considered it a moment. "Some of both, I think," she said. "About half and half."

"Oh. Well . . . okay." Kira paused. "Laren . . ."

"Yeah, Nerys?"

"Watch your back, okay?"

Ro smiled. "Why? Are you going to come gunning for it?"

Kira smiled back at her. "Don't worry. Even if I do, my aim has been known to go bad from time to time."

The Maquis nodded, turned again, and walked away.

Sisko had visited the so-called Bajoran Chamber before, when he first came to *Deep Space Nine.* It was a large high-ceilinged room, dominated by a semi-circular podium. There were nine seats on the podium, the one in the middle belonging to the head of the provisional government.

At one point, it had looked as if that might be Kai Winn. And what a disaster that would have been, he mused, as he watched the tall imposing form of First Minister Shakaar enter the room.

The eight other officials that sat on the planetary council filed in behind him, one by one. And one by one, they took their seats on the podium.

Ompar Tenzil was conspicuous by his absence. His seat on the council had been taken by another individual from his province.

Kira leaned toward Sisko and whispered, "They don't look very happy, do they?"

"No," agreed the captain, "they don't."

But that was hardly a surprise. When one's entire civilization was placed in jeopardy, one tended to look harshly on those who were to blame for it. To say the least.

Jake, who was standing on Sisko's other side, heaved a sigh. "What do you think they'll do to her?" he asked.

The captain shook his head. "I'm afraid I don't know."

It was only after all the ministers had composed themselves that a door opened on the other side of the chamber—and Varis Sul walked in, flanked by a couple of Bajoran security officers. In Sisko's eyes, Varis looked like a child in the company of hard-eyed adults.

Of course, that wasn't too far from the truth. Despite the responsibilities she had taken upon herself, the girl was a little older than Jake.

But it wasn't for that reason alone that the captain hoped the council would be lenient. It was because whatever crimes Varis had committed, she'd only acted out of concern for her people.

As Varis came to a stop before Shakaar, who sat at the center of the semicircle, she raised her eyes to him. Despite the seriousness of her situation, she didn't waver. She didn't make a sound. She just stood there and waited for First Minister Shakaar to address her.

Shakaar didn't keep her waiting. "This council has convened," he announced to all present, including the sprinkling of interested spectators standing around the chamber, "to decide the fate of Varis Sul, tetrarch of Paqu Village." He lowered his eyes to meet the girl's. "Do you understand the charges brought against you?" he asked.

Varis nodded. "I do. I am charged with endangering the lives of my people—the very thing I was sworn to protect. I am charged with dealing in the black market, which stands contrary to the interests of Bajor. And, lastly, I am charged with defying the authority of the provisional government."

"That about sums it up," Kira remarked.

Jake didn't say anything. He just looked worried.

Shakaar considered the young tetrarch. "And do you deny any of these charges? Have you anything to say in your defense?"

Varis shook her head. "Nothing," she told him. "I am guilty—and I will accept whatever punishment this council sees fit to inflict upon me."

Sisko sighed. It was clear that the youngster had learned her lesson. Unfortunately, that might not be enough.

Shakaar turned from Varis and addressed the onlookers. "What of you witnesses? Have you anything to say on behalf of the accused?"

It was a rhetorical question, a vestige of older forms of trial that no longer survived on Bajor. No one expected an answer, least of all Shakaar.

The captain hadn't expected one, either. So he was as surprised as anyone when it came from his own mouth.

"I would like to speak on Varis Sul's behalf," he replied, in a loud but even voice. "Even if she will not speak for herself."

Shakaar looked at him. So did the rest of the council, and Kira, and Jake. And so, at last, did the accused.

"I am grateful," she told him. "But this is unnecessary."

"No," Sisko said, stepping forward to separate himself from the other onlookers. "I think this is very necessary."

"Go, Dad," Jake whispered.

Shakaar made a gesture of invitation to him. "By all means, Captain Sisko—speak."

The captain gathered his thoughts before he started. After all, Varis's life might be changed by what he had to say.

"The one on trial here," he began, "is Varis Sul, tetrarch of Paqu village. However, she is only partly responsible for the chain of events that placed Bajor in jeopardy and flaunted the authority of the government."

One of the secondary ministers leaned forward. "Are you saying that we should charge someone else with these crimes, in addition to Varis?"

"I am," Sisko replied. "And that someone, I think, is *you.*"

The minister looked aghast. "Me? What are you saying?" Suddenly pale, he looked around at the others on the council. "I assure you, I did nothing wrong."

But his peers looked uneasy. No doubt, they were thinking of Ompar Tenzil, and wondering how many of him there might be.

"Perhaps not as an individual," the captain went on, pleased to have achieved the desired effect. "However, as a member of the council, you are as guilty as anyone else for the marginal and sometimes even miserable conditions that still prevail on this world."

"That's ridiculous," muttered another of the ministers—this one a female. "We've dedicated our lives to the restoration of Bajor."

"But to what effect?" Sisko asked her. "This government is riddled with power-brokers and profit-seekers. Perhaps you yourself have committed no crimes, but you've allowed others to do so. Otherwise, how could the black market have thrived—at the expense of the population? How could a few greedy men have achieved control over such vast resources?"

"In other words," said Shakaar, unperturbed, "we on the council created an onerous set of conditions—if not directly, then indirectly. And given those conditions, Varis had no choice but to break our laws."

The captain eyed the first minister. Shakaar was nobody's fool, he mused. But then, he'd known that for some time already.

"Of course she had a choice," Sisko conceded. "I'm not saying Varis had no part in this. But if you folks had been doing your jobs, she never would've had to consider buying replicators on the black market—and Bajor would never have been plagued with that virus."

Shakaar nodded. "Thank you, Captain. I, for one, will take those words to heart. What's more, given my own history, I can't help but sympathize with someone who breaks a couple of laws—especially when it's to keep her people from falling prey to starvation."

Abruptly his demeanor changed. Sisko wasn't sure what tipped him off to it—a hardening of the man's jawline, perhaps, or a subtle crease in the skin between his eyes. It didn't matter. What *did* matter was he knew he'd lost his plea for leniency.

"However," Shakaar continued, "we can't run the risk of someone doing what Varis did. This time, we were lucky. Next time, all of Bajor may pay the price."

"Merciful Prophets," Kira whispered. "He's going to banish her."

The captain glanced at his first officer. Her face was ashen.

"Therefore," said the first minister, "I have no choice but to strip this woman of her title as tetrarch—and exile her from Bajor for the rest of her natural life."

Varis shuddered, as if she were naked and a chill wind had blown through the room. It seemed to Sisko that she'd expected a lesser punishment to be handed down, despite her willingness to accept whatever she received.

So had they all, he reflected sadly.

"No," Jake moaned. He turned to his father. "They can't do that to her, Dad. It's not right. Varis thought she was doing something good. She wasn't trying to hurt anybody."

"I know," said the captain. But it didn't change anything.

"I beg your pardon," came a muted voice from beyond the chamber, "but I do not believe the Prophets would approve of this decision."

All heads turned toward the door through which Varis had entered. A moment later, no less a dignitary than Kai Winn crossed its threshold and glided into the chamber. Her face, as always, was a mask of serenity, betraying none of the emotions working inside her.

Shakaar stood. So did the rest of the council, not wishing to appear disrespectful of the Kai—no matter what they may have thought of her personally.

"We are honored by your presence," said the first minister, bowing his head ever so slightly. "And curious to know why the Prophets would voice an opinion in this matter."

"The Prophets have *not* voiced an opinion," Winn replied, her pale blue eyes unwavering in their scrutiny. "As Kai, however, I am qualified to remark on what their opinion would be. And I can tell you, they would not be happy to see Varis Sul banished from her homeworld."

Careful not to rush and thereby dispel the illusion of inner calm, Winn moved to the girl's side and placed her hand on Varis's cheek. The tetrarch obviously didn't know what to say. The Kai was possibly the last person she had counted on as an ally.

"Have no fear, child," Winn assured her. "Trust in the Prophets and they will guide you to your salvation."

The girl shook her head. "I'm not worthy of the

Prophets' assistance," she answered. "I'm guilty. I must be punished."

The Kai smiled her most benevolent smile. It never ceased to amaze Sisko that so many Bajorans actually believed in the woman's sincerity—when it was so clear to *him* she was merely pursuing her own agenda.

And what agenda was she pursuing now, in defending the tetrarch? The captain wasn't quite sure. At least, not yet.

"Don't presume to know more than the Prophets," Winn told Varis. "Guilt and innocence," she continued, casting a meaningful glance at the council, "is only for *them* to decide."

"Tell me," Shakaar said, his eyes fixed on the imposing figure of the Kai. "What would the Prophets have us do in this instance? Are we to stand by and watch as our laws are flaunted? As our people are placed in grave danger?"

Winn's smile broadened. "Laws are made by men, First Minister. They are only our humble attempts to interpret the morality imparted to us by the Prophets." She gazed lovingly at Varis—or so it seemed. "What we must strive for is not law, but justice. And it would not be just to exile this child when her only purpose was to help her people."

Shakaar appeared to be mulling the Kai's words. "Then you would see her go free, unrepentant of her crimes?" he asked.

Winn shrugged. "I think Varis Sul is already repentant," she observed.

"But surely," the first minister maintained, "an atonement—"

"If you insist on an atonement," the Kai interrupted, "let it be a religious one. She will perform holy acts for a period of five years, under my scrutiny. By then, I believe, she will have embraced the maturity and the wisdom a tetrarch needs to govern her people."

"And in the meantime, who will serve as tetrarch in Paqu village?" one of the other councilors inquired.

"Why," Winn said, *"she* will. Don't forget, Etran Dol, I will be watching her every step of the way."

Shakaar frowned. He could hardly argue with the Kai when she had taken such a firm and public stand. What's more, her arguments seemed so *reasonable*.

"Very well, then," he declared. "It shall be as Kai Winn recommends. Varis Sul will remain tetrarch of Paqu village—under the Kai's scrutiny." He turned to the other councilors. "This tribunal is adjourned."

Jake laughed. "I can't believe it," he said. "Varis is free." He turned to his father. "And of all people, Kai Winn was the one who rescued her."

"Yes," Sisko said. "Of all people."

As the Kai turned to depart the chamber, leaving Varis too numb to know if she should laugh or cry, she glanced in the captain's direction. There was a look of triumph on her face—so subtle that one might have missed it, unless one knew what to look for.

In the end, Winn seemed to say, *I always find a way to win. After all, I am the Kai.*

And she *had* won, hadn't she? Or . . .

"Damn," Sisko blurted appreciatively. "That was masterful. Absolutely masterful."

Jake looked at him. "What was, Dad?"

"I'll tell you later," the captain responded. "Right now, Varis needs a friend. If I were you, I'd help her put what happened here into some kind of perspective."

His son nodded. "I hear you, Dad." And with that, he made a beeline for the tetrarch.

"You know," Kira said, "Shakaar had me going for a minute there."

Sisko eyed her. "Me, too. I really believed he wanted to exile Varis."

"While all along," the major continued, "he was playing a shrewd little game."

"If he allowed the tetrarch to go free," the captain remarked, "he would've met with considerable opposition. And the Kai could have taken advantage of that."

"You're not kidding," Kira agreed. "She would've screamed up and down that he was being too lenient. That he wasn't acting responsibly as first minister."

"Therefore, he appeared to lower the boom on poor Varis," Sisko observed, "knowing all the while that Winn would attend this event. And knowing also that she would oppose whatever he did."

The major smiled. "That's our Shakaar. He managed to get the girl off the hook, yet avoid the appearance of leniency. And the Kai feels like she won one, which will make her a little less dangerous for a while. A nice job all around."

The captain grunted. "You're not the least bit worried that Winn will unduly influence Varis? With all that scrutiny she was talking about . . ."

Kira waved away the suggestion. "Don't believe a word of it. The last thing the Kai wants to do is spend her time in Paqu village, overseeing the daily activities of a young girl she doesn't particularly like. She'd much rather be in the capitol, stirring up trouble."

Sisko smiled at the thought. "Yes," he said. "I suppose she would."

CHAPTER 18

VARIS EMBRACED JAKE so hard he thought his ribs were going to crack. Then she turned to face his father.

"You were wonderful," the tetrarch gushed. "The things that you said . . ."

"The things I said," Sisko rumbled, "were for the purpose of getting you out of the trouble you'd gotten yourself into. I did that out of respect for your basically decent motivations"—he glanced at Jake—"and your long-standing relationship with my son. But understand—I can defend your actions without approving of them."

Varis took a step back and quietly said, "I see."

"No, I don't think you do," said the captain. "To be tetrarch, you have to lead with both your heart and your head. Think too much and you become paralyzed, unable to make a decision. But follow your emotions exclusively, yield to your impulses, and you can unwittingly cause disaster . . ."

"Which is what I did," she admitted.

"C'mon Dad," Jake said uncomfortably, "Ease up."

"No," Varis told him. "No, he's right, Jake. Even if everything had worked out, even if there had been no plague . . . my actions still validated the black market, and put myself and my people at risk. As it is, people died because of me.

"I can try to foist the blame off as much as possible. Blame the government, blame the Prophets, blame whomever. But ultimately, at the end of the day when I look in the mirror, the blame for what happened and for the deaths that occurred rest squarely on the person whose reflection I'm staring at. How can I deny that to you and your father? I can't even deny it to myself."

She sighed heavily. "And despite all the punishment I've endured, it will never be enough to cleanse my soul of the deaths that will always be on it."

"But you can't let that knowledge destroy you," Sisko said. "It's far too easy to curl up into a ball and avoid dealing with the difficulties thrust upon you. Believe me . . . I know."

"Don't worry, Captain," Varis told him. "I won't run. And I won't end it all, the way that poor devil Ompar did. I'll use what I've learned to be a better, wiser tetrarch. But a happy one?" She shook her head, a shadow crossing her face. "That, I fear, I will never be."

Jake wanted to say something to comfort her—but what could he say? What could anyone say?

With his father's hand on his shoulder, he watched Varis walk away into the distance, heading back to the home she wanted so desperately to help—and in the attempt, nearly destroyed.

"Absolutely not!" Quark cried.

Morn looked at him from across the bar, his hands held apart in an appeal for fairness—for reason. Still, the Ferengi was adamant.

After all, a drink on the house was sometimes useful for building goodwill. But an unlimited number of free drinks for a lush like Morn could break even the most robust establishment.

"Listen," Quark said, poking a finger at Morn, "whatever agreement you made was with my no-good scheming brother." He glowered sidelong at Rom, who was cringing in a corner. "As I understand it," Quark went on, "this place wasn't even operating under my name at the time the deal was struck. So if you've got a complaint, take it to the proprietor of Rom's Pleasure Palace!"

Morn glanced at Rom. The Ferengi shrugged helplessly. Obviously, Rom didn't have the wherewithal to make good on the promise.

Besides, the offer hadn't been made to further Rom's fortune—only to encourage Morn to save his own life. Surely, Quark thought, Morn would see that and forgive the debt.

As it turned out, the bartender was right. With a sigh that smacked only slightly of annoyance, Morn got up from his bar stool and meandered out into the flow of traffic on the Promenade.

But he would be back, Quark told himself—just as soon as he got thirsty. Morn had a notoriously short memory when his recollections interfered with his creature comforts.

The Ferengi looked at his brother, who was still cringing. "Well," he said, "that's another fine mess I've gotten you out of."

Rom nodded appreciatively. "Yes, Brother."

"Not that I should have anything to do with you," Quark went on, "considering you hijacked my bar as soon as I was gone."

"Yes, Brother," Rom agreed, wincing.

"On the other hand," said the bartender, "were our situations reversed, I would've done the exact same thing—so I can hardly hold it against you."

Rom smiled and straightened a little. "I'm glad you see it that way, Brother. *Very* glad."

Quark grunted. "Good. Now go check on that shipment I arranged for back on Mephil Trantos. I want to make sure I got everything I contracted for."

The other Ferengi nodded vigorously. "Yes, Brother. And thank you."

Quark dismissed him with a sweep of his hand. "Just don't let it happen again, all right?"

Rom had barely descended into the storage space beneath the bar when Odo entered the place. The constable had that predatory look on his face that always made the bartender a little uneasy.

"Well," Quark said, rubbing his hands together and smiling, "what can I do for you today, Odo?"

The shapeshifter frowned. "You can tell me what was in that shipment you received a few hours ago."

The Ferengi pretended to think for a moment. "Shipment?" he repeated.

Odo's frown deepened into a scowl. "Don't be coy with me, Quark. According to the manifest, you got a container full of Hanipharri brandy."

Quark stroked his chin. "Ah, *that* shipment. How could I have forgotten?"

"The problem," said the constable, "is that the stuff arrived on a Metileusan cargo ship—and the Metileusans stopped dealing with the Hanipharri several months ago. Which means you've received something else entirely."

The Ferengi swallowed. "By the Nagus . . . I've been swindled!"

Odo harrumphed. "Not likely." He leaned forward over the bar. "If I were to guess, I'd say you made some sort of deal out there in Orion territory—for some sort of contraband, perhaps."

Quark shook his head. "It's nothing like that, I swear it. I only—"

"What seems to be the trouble here?" came a deep voice.

Both of them turned to see Sisko, who was entering Quark's Place from the Promenade. Sisko had a bemused expression on his face. He'd been in a good mood ever since his return from Bajor.

"Our friend here," the constable began, "has been trying to pull the wool over our eyes. *Again.*"

The captain looked at the Ferengi. "Is this true, Quark?"

The bartender saw he had no chance of slipping the hook. "All right," he admitted. "Maybe I tried to avoid a few small duties here and there—"

"By dealing with the Orions?" Sisko asked.

Inwardly, Quark squirmed. "Er . . . now that you mention it . . ."

"After I warned you about that sort of thing?" the captain pressed.

"But I didn't accept delivery until after we got back," the Ferengi pointed out.

"A subtle difference," Sisko noted.

"But a difference nonetheless," Quark insisted. "And I might point out that there was nothing illegal about what I obtained."

"I'll believe that when I see it for myself," Odo returned.

"If that's what it takes." Quark sighed and led them downstairs to his storage chamber.

They found Rom going through the shipment in question. As soon as he caught sight of Sisko and the constable, he tried to put everything back in the cargo container.

"Don't bother," Quark said.

Rom backed off from the stuff. "Er . . . whatever you say, Brother."

The shapeshifter knelt in front of the pile Rom had made. His eyes narrowed as he inspected the goods, a collection of timeworn implements from a variety of cultures.

"Well," he said, unable to keep a note of surprise out of his voice, "how about that?" He looked up at Sisko. "It's true—there doesn't seem to be anything illegal here. Just an assortment of collectibles—for which some dealer will no doubt pay a healthy sum."

True, thought Quark. At least, that's what his trading partner had claimed back on Mephil Trantos.

The human took a closer look at the pile as well. "What's this?" he asked, and pulled a wooden club out.

Quark shrugged. "It's called a Loo-ee-vil something-or-other. The Orion I got it from didn't know what it was for. He just threw it in with all the other merchandise."

Sisko nodded. "I see." He glanced at the Ferengi.

And Quark saw the *look*—the one that he had trained himself to notice, the one that told him a customer was in love with something he had for sale. Except, in this instance, the Ferengi had more to gain by giving the thing away than by selling it. Besides, how much could it have been worth?

"Why don't you take that," he suggested, "as a gift?"

Sisko regarded him. "I'm touched, Quark."

The Ferengi smiled magnanimously. "Think of it as a confirmation of the bond between two comrades."

"All right," Sisko agreed. "I'll do that. Incidentally, Quark—you have some duties to pay."

"Quite a few," Odo added. "A rather large sum, no doubt."

The Ferengi would have been worried—except for the "gift" he had just given the station's commanding officer. "Surely," he said, "this is something two comrades ought to be able to work out."

Sisko smiled. "I thought we already had."

Suddenly Quark felt a good deal less sure of himself. "But what about the good deed I did? If not for me, Major Kira and her friends would never have uncovered those corrupt Bajorans."

Sisko rested the club on his shoulder and looked at the constable. "That's true, isn't it?"

"I suppose so," Odo replied.

The human held up a finger. "I've got an idea. Let's waive the jail time."

"Jail time?" Quark repeated.

The shapeshifter sighed. "I hate to do that," he said. "But under the circumstances, I guess I can make an exception."

Sisko nodded. "Then it seems we're done here, Constable." He turned to the bartender. "See you, Quark."

As the Starfleet officer and the shapeshifter ascended the stairs that led back up to the bar, the bartender cursed beneath his breath. Sisko wouldn't have seen him prosecuted in any case, club or no club. He had been tricked into giving the thing away for nothing, even if it wasn't worth much more than that—and it hurt.

Rom came over to him, smiling. "Isn't that terrific?" he said. "The captain is so grateful for what you did, he's not going to put you in jail."

Quark glared at him. "Shut up, Rom."

The other Ferengi winced. "Yes, Brother."

Sisko leaned back in his chair, ignoring the monitor on his desk and all the duties it represented, and took a moment to enjoy himself. After all, it wasn't every day he came across one of *these*.

He balanced the Louisville Slugger on the palms of his hands, supporting it by its extremities. He considered the weight of it, the shape, the texture of the wood. For all the chemicals that had gone into its preservation, it felt just as authentic as the bats he used in his holodeck recreations.

There was only one disparity. In the holodeck, the bats only *felt* real. This one *was* real. It made a world of difference.

A moment later, he heard the mechanical hum and the grinding of gears that accompanied the opening and closing of the Cardassian-designed doors to his office. But he didn't look up. At least, not right away.

"Uh . . . what's that?" came a familiar voice.

"A bat," he replied softly, still deep in the throes of admiration.

"A bat?" his visitor echoed.

"A bat," he said again. "Just a bat."

There was a pause. "I don't get it," said the newcomer.

That's when he looked up—and regarded the bemused expression on the face of his first officer. While Kira knew of the captain's affection for the pastime, she had never actually seen him participate in it.

More's the pity, he thought. You never really know a man until you've seen him rounding third, heading for home. But that was another conversation entirely.

"An interesting thing," he began. "The game of baseball, I mean. Back in the old days, on Earth, we used to spend a lot of time glorifying certain players. Babe Ruth, for instance. Cy Young. And in my case—"

"Buck Bokai," Kira said.

Sisko looked at her. "How did you know that?" he inquired.

She shrugged. "I remember those aliens using his image to learn about humans. Not something easily forgotten."

He smiled. "Of course. You see, the central drama in baseball is an individual contest—that of batter versus pitcher. Pitcher versus batter. One on one, strength and guile versus strength and guile."

He turned the bat around in his hands so that he could grip the handle. Wrapping his fingers around the slender wooden shaft, he felt each scar and pit and scratch—and reveled in them. Then he took a little practice swing, just for the hell of it.

The Bajoran smiled her endearing, almost impish, smile. "That's very interesting. But I'm assuming there's another reason you called me in here."

"Indeed, there is," Sisko said—and went on just as if she'd never spoken, as if she hadn't even entered the room. "Baseball was a series of individual contests," he ruminated. "And whoever won the majority of these individual contests generally won the game. However, that's an oversimplification of it."

"I see," Kira said, though she probably didn't see at all. Not yet, anyway. She was just trying to speed things up.

But some things resisted being sped up. Some things took their own sweet time.

"An oversimplification," he explained, "because none of those individual contests took place in a vacuum. There might have been men on base, which would change the way the pitcher executed his wind-up. Or there might have been a couple of sluggers behind this particular batter, which meant the pitcher didn't have the luxury of nibbling around the strike zone.

"And on the pitcher's side, there were eight men or women playing the field for him. They knew the hitter's strengths and weaknesses, and they knew how the pitcher was going to pitch, and they would do their best to conform to these conditions. Without a good defense behind him, even a good pitcher might not do very well."

The Bajoran sighed. "Are we getting anywhere near the moral, sir?"

"We're almost there," he assured her. "The point is, we can't always pick our partners. But we can play with them. And if we put our minds to it, we can be one hell of a team." He laid the barrel of the bat on his shoulder. "You and Ro," he told her, "were one hell of a team."

Kira nodded judiciously. "We were at that." She paused. "Then you don't mind the fact that we let her return to the Maquis?"

"I mind a great deal," the captain remarked. "But without Ro, we might have lost this game. I figure we owe her something for that."

His first officer folded her arms across her chest. "Is that what you're going to tell Starfleet Command? That we had one of the most notorious of the Maquis right in our hands—and we let her go?"

"Actually," Sisko said, "I was planning on blaming it all on you."

Kira's brow creased. "On me?"

"That's correct," he told her. "You're a Bajoran. They can't discipline you the way they would me. And the Federation wants too much to maintain good relations with your people to make an incident out of a small . . . what shall we call it?"

"Misunderstanding," his first officer suggested.

The captain pointed the bat at her. "Exactly."

"So I'm your scapegoat?" Kira asked.

Sisko grinned. "Not at all. The fact is, you *did* let Ro get away. I'd say you ought to take some responsibility for that."

The Bajoran frowned. "Fine. I'll . . . er, go to *bat* for you, if it means we don't have to look for another Emissary."

He nodded appreciatively. "I like your choice of metaphor, Major."

She grunted. "I thought you would."

Suddenly the captain realized something was different. He pointed to Kira's ear.

"Major," he said, "that ornament . . ."

"Yes, sir?"

"That's not yours."

"No, sir. I found it waiting for me in my quarters when I returned. A . . . friend . . . left it there."

"I see," Sisko said. "Do I happen to know this friend?"

Kira sighed. "Sir . . . in a way, I don't think anybody knows her."

And with that, she exited his office.

The captain watched her go for a moment, then turned reluctantly to his monitor. After all, civilizations could grow and wane, planets could break loose of their orbits and spin into their suns, and no one at Starfleet would raise an eyebrow. In time, they would even forgive him his dealings with Ro Laren.

But God help him if the monthly reports came in late.

As O'Brien and his family emerged from Garak's tailor shop onto the Promenade, the chief noted that the "Rom's" sign across the way had been taken down, and the "Quark's" sign put back up.

Freed from Garak's, Molly skipped ahead of her parents, twirling about in a new dress that shimmered in the subdued lighting. The little girl seemed thoroughly unfazed by her sickness, from which she had only recently recovered.

Yes, she was still easily fatigued and her appetite was not what it should have been. But Bashir had assured O'Brien and his wife that Molly would improve in both respects. And his word was good enough for them.

"You know, Mrs. O'Brien," Garak said from the doorway, "I don't recall the sound of laughter on the Promenade when this station was called *Tarok Nor*. It is not as unappealing as I was led to believe."

Keiko turned, her arm still wrapped around Miles, and shot Garak a proud mother's smile. "Good," she said, "because I intend for there to be a lot more laughter around here."

Garak's eyes gleamed. He tilted his head. "Then I take it you will be here more often."

Keiko glanced at her husband. "I'm not going anywhere for a long time," she replied.

"I'll second that," said the chief.

Leaving Garak behind on his doorstep, O'Brien led his family in the direction of the replimat. On the way, Molly continued to remain a good ten feet ahead of them, spinning like a tiny ballerina. She looked positively luminescent in her dress as it caught the light.

Unfortunately, Molly wasn't watching where she was going. Before O'Brien could warn her, she spun right into the tall figure of Captain Sisko. The impact caused her to stumble, but the captain's strong arm caught her and then hefted the little girl into the air.

"Let me down!" Molly cried. "Let me down!" But she was giggling mightily the whole time.

Sisko broke into a smile of his own as he turned to O'Brien. "Lose something, Chief?"

O'Brien noted that the captain's ribs had fully healed, or he could never have lifted Molly that way. "Not at all, sir," he replied. "Sorry about that."

Sisko studied the chief's daughter, then lowered her gently to the ground. "She's getting her color back," he noted, as Molly ran to her mother's arms. "She's making good progress, I take it?"

"Getting stronger by the day," Keiko replied, as she lifted Molly. "And wearing me out."

The captain nodded approvingly. "That's the kind of news I like to hear." He turned to O'Brien. "Welcome back, Chief." Then he addressed Keiko again. "That goes for all of you."

With that, he headed for his office in Ops. O'Brien watched him go, then took Keiko's hand and resumed their journey toward the replimat.

It had been kind of Sisko, the chief thought, to give the command crew some much-needed time off with their mission successfully completed. He certainly relished the idea of a day or two without any pressures of any sort—or anyway, the kind that could be foreseen. He could do without isolinear chips and fused wires for a while.

A moment later, he and his family rounded the last

corner to the replimat. As Molly eagerly began scouting out a table for the three of them, O'Brien started wondering about what to order for her. Perhaps it was time for her to try something from one of the more exotic worlds.

His thoughts were interrupted when he spotted Dax across the way, getting up from her own table, her meal completed. She smiled at the sight of the chief and his family.

Abruptly O'Brien realized he had something to say to her. He glanced at Keiko and said, "Excuse me, will you? I won't be more than a second or two, I promise."

His wife chuckled. "A second or two. I'll hold you to that."

The chief wove his way through the tables toward Dax. As he approached, he got her attention.

"Chief?" she said.

O'Brien sighed. "I've a confession to make," he admitted. "Back in the captain's office, just before you remembered—"

Dax held up a hand. "You don't have to say it. I was there, remember? You were about to ask for permission to leave the station."

The chief frowned. "Not exactly. The truth is I was going to resign from Starfleet. Hand over my uniform and get down to Bajor any way I could."

The Trill looked at him. "I see. And?"

"And I wanted to tell you it would've been the wrong decision. If I'd left as I intended, that problem on level seven might've gotten out of hand. The infirmary might've been affected. And you might never have developed the cure."

Dax thought about that for a moment. "There's no need for an apology," she said finally. "We Trills have an expression—at forty, you think you know everything. At four hundred, you realize you know nothing." She shrugged. "Anybody can make a mistake. Don't beat yourself up about it."

O'Brien smiled. "Thanks."

His eyes locked with Dax's for a moment. And for the first time, he saw the depth of wisdom in those eyes. They were ancient eyes, full of knowledge and delight in the learning of it. Eyes that wanted to see everything they could.

But he could also tell that those eyes had known pain and mourning. And that they had cried only recently.

He nodded in acknowledgment of the bond between them—the bond of what it meant to be a parent. It gave them a common ground—a new way of learning from each other. O'Brien looked forward to it.

Then he remembered that his family was waiting for him. "I'll see you later," he told the Trill.

"Later," she agreed.

As the chief made his way back through the replimat, he took in the sight of his wife and child, and a feeling of completeness settled over him. It was a feeling he wanted to preserve forever.

Look for STAR TREK Fiction from Pocket Books

Star Trek®: The Original Series

Star Trek: The Next Generation®

Star Trek: Deep Space Nine®

The Search • Diane Carey
Warped • K. W. Jeter
The Way of the Warrior • Diane Carey
Star Trek: Klingon • Dean W. Smith & Kristine K. Rusch

Star Trek: Voyager®

Flashback • Diane Carey

Coming Next Month from Pocket Books

STAR TREK®

MIND-MELD
by
John Vornholt

**Please turn the page for a
preview of *Mind-Meld*. . . .**

In the Sundial Visitors' Lodge, Spock rose to his feet, walked to the doorway, and peered into the darkness. If he were a human, he might be accused of pacing nervously, so he tried to think of a logical reason to leave the bridge and check on Teska. He had heard some childlike shouts, but he wasn't sure if they came from outside or from one of the back rooms. Suddenly, the forty-six minutes they had to spend on Rigel V seemed like a very long time.

Behind him, McCoy laughed at the antics of Oblek, who had proven to be an adroit juggler as well as a jovial host. Kirk and Spock were nursing their first glasses of ale, and Kirk glanced sympathetically at him. Spock remembered that his friend had been a parent, even if he had never watched his son grow up. If unwarranted concern was part of being a parent, he was glad that he had been spared such unpleasantness.

Oblek noticed that he was losing his audience, and he dropped the four sacks of seed he had been juggling. They hit the floor and spilled open.

"Hey!" the proprietor cried. "We don't pay you to make a mess around here, Oblek."

"Sorry," said the prefect, looking crestfallen.

Kirk slapped his hands on his thighs and stood up. "I think it is time to be going. We can beam up from here. Spock, you *are* the only one with any money."

"This is all I have," said Spock, handing a stack of coins to the proprietor. "Will that be sufficient?"

"Oh, my, yes!" said the man with a big grin on his face. "Half of that would be enough."

As he returned a few coins to the Vulcan, the man's face dissolved into shock, and he stared past Spock. The Vulcan whirled around at the same time the others did, to see the cause of his alarm.

Standing in the doorway was little Teska, with a vacant look on her face and covered in blood.

Kirk rushed to the girl's side. "What happened to you?"

McCoy was right behind Kirk, and he opened a small medical pouch on his belt and took out a diagnostic instrument. Despite the blood all over her clothes, she didn't appear injured.

"She's suffered some kind of trauma," said McCoy. "Alert sickbay, Jim, and tell them we're on our way."

"No!" said Teska forcefully, as if snapping out of a trance. "I am not hurt. But Ambassador Denker's dead."

Prefect Oblek gasped and sank down into one of the seedy chairs. "Denker is dead?"

"Murdered." The girl looked up at Spock. "I did not intend to do it, but he was dying."

"Do what?" asked Kirk. "What did you do?"

Spock's jaw tightened. "You performed a mind-meld."

The girl nodded. "I saw it all. They argued, and Denker walked off. Vitra sent Mondral after him, and they fought. Mondral stuck a knife in his throat."

"You *saw* this?" asked Oblek, amazed.

"Yes."

"No," said Spock. "She did not actually witness the murder. But she did a mind-meld with Denker, and she shared *his* vision of it. Is that right, Teska?"

The girl nodded vacantly.

Oblek shook his head, confused. "What is a *mind-meld?*"

Kirk looked at Spock and sighed. If anybody was going to have to explain the Vulcan mind-meld, it would be Spock.

"Wait a minute," said McCoy, "maybe Teska is mistaken. Maybe the man is still alive." He was headed out the door when they heard shouts and running footsteps coming closer.

The girl suddenly jerked her head and looked outside, as if reminded of something. "I know *why* he did it, too. So Denker could not tell the Assembly about Vitra's illegal activities. Denker refused to falsify his report."

"Let me note the time," said Oblek, fumbling in his pocket for a timepiece.

"I want to see the body," insisted McCoy. Before he could get out the door, two Rigelians ran up to the doorway, shouting, "Prefect! Prefect! There's been a murder!"

"Yes, I know," grumbled the pudgy bureaucrat. "Ambassador Denker."

The Rigelians looked at each other in amazement. "That's right. But we just found his body."

"Are you sure he's dead?" asked McCoy.

"I think so," said one of them. Then his eyes trailed down to the blood-covered girl, and he gasped. "Was it *her?*"

The prefect muscled past Spock and Kirk and headed for the door, with McCoy in pursuit. "Don't anybody jump to conclusions. We have a witness, I think. I'm not really sure."

"Prefect, we can appreciate your difficulty, but we must return," said Kirk.

"She cannot leave!" growled the prefect. "Not until there's an inquest." He turned to the proprietor. "Give them all beds for the night, at city expense. And don't let that little girl out of your sight."

As Oblek and McCoy rushed off with the others to examine the body, the proprietor crossed his arms and stared at his unexpected guests. He didn't look very happy, and neither did Captain Kirk.

Spock picked up a cloth napkin and began to dab the blood from Teska's face. "Do you have some clean clothes that would fit her?"

"Yes," admitted the man. He turned to the woman standing motionless in the curtained doorway. "Clothes for the child," he ordered. She rushed off, sending the beads clattering.

Kirk bent down and whispered to Spock, "We can't stay here. We'll miss our rendezvous on Vulcan."

"I know," replied Spock, still cleaning Teska. "But we cannot ignore the laws of a member world of the Federation."

The proprietor moved closer to them. "What are you two talking about?"

"We understand the need for Teska to testify," said Kirk, "but the *Enterprise* is on a mission. How soon will the inquest be?"

"Can't be until tomorrow at the earliest," answered the man. "We need a balance of twenty-six men and twenty-six women to hear her testimony. And we have to have numerologists examine the body."

Spock said nothing. It was important to bring a murderer to justice, but his main concern was Teska. Frowning, he gazed into her eyes. "Are you in any discomfort?"

She paused as if taking inventory, then shook her head. "I am well. I was taken aback at first—there was a knife in his throat. I called for help, but no one came. He was dying, and he wanted so badly to speak to me. Did I do wrong, Uncle?"

"No, you behaved logically. However, if we are delayed, your *koon-ut-la* will be delayed. The ramifications of that are unknown."

Teska swallowed hard and looked down at the floor. "I was not thinking clearly."

The Rigelian woman returned from the back of the lodge with a stack of black clothes. She handed them to Teska and gave her a sympathetic smile. "Come with me. I'll take you to a room where you can change."

"Don't let her out of your sight," warned the proprietor.

As the two females filed out of the room, Kirk slumped into a chair and drained his glass of ale. "What are we going to do, Spock?"

The Vulcan cocked his head. "It would appear that we will spend the night on Rigel V."

A moment later, McCoy shuffled back into the lodge, shaking his head. "He's dead, Jim."

"Any evidence that would help to back up Teska's story?" asked Kirk.

"Well, the knife is very crude—homemade with a wooden handle—but it did the job. The only way Denker was going to communicate with anyone was through a mind-meld. I can't speak for the Rigelians, but Teska's story certainly sounds plausible to me."

"Several times he mentioned a report he was working on," said Spock. "Has anyone found those documents?"

"The prefect is looking for his luggage now, and he's also trying to round up Vitra and Mondral. Apparently, the three of them were staying at a different visitors' lodge, farther up the hill. No other witnesses have come forward, other than Teska."

"Who is not really a witness," muttered Kirk. He jumped to his feet, looking anxious to take some sort of action. "I've got to report this to Sarek. Bones, let's go back to the ship."

"Oh, no," said the anxious proprietor, "you're not allowed to leave!"

"No, the girl is not allowed to leave. I have a job to do." The captain activated his wrist communicator. "Kirk to *Enterprise*. Two to beam up."

The Rigelian proprietor was still sputtering in anger as McCoy and Kirk disappeared. He put his hands on his hips. "Does he always do exactly what he wants to do?"

"Under most circumstances," answered Spock.

The Rigelian woman entered through the curtain and approached Spock. "After she put on the clothes, she lay down on the bed and went to sleep instantly."

"That is to be expected," said Spock. "Do not wake her."

"And you?" asked the proprietor. "Do you want a room?"

"No," said the Vulcan, sitting in one of the decrepit chairs. "This will be sufficient."

"Suit yourself. It's going to be a long night."

Of that, Spock had no doubt.

Spock was awakened from a light sleep by a chirp on his wrist communicator. He sat up, feeling twinges of stiffness in his back, and activated the device. "Spock here."

"Kirk here," said the captain's voice. "Any new developments?"

Spock looked around the dreary foyer, which was even drearier now that several lights in the doorway had been extinguished. From the silence, darkness, and the coolness of the breeze that wafted through the open door, he judged it to be the middle of the night on Rigel V.

"No developments," he answered. "But then, I haven't spoken to anyone recently."

"Well," said the captain, "we may have gotten a break, along with a tragedy. Can I speak freely?"

"I am alone."

Kirk went on. "I've spoken to Sarek, and the Romulans have had their share of problems, too. The boy's father was killed when his shuttlecraft was destroyed by a Romulan border patrol."

"Is the boy safe?" asked Spock.

"Yes. This apparently happened *after* the boy's father turned him over to Pardek. The boy doesn't even know his father is dead. And now Pardek is afraid to venture very far into Federation space in a Romulan scout ship, and I can't say I blame him. They're hiding out in the Duperre Asteroid Belt, and they've requested that we escort them to Vulcan."

Spock lifted an eyebrow. "I see. Then a delay of a few days will not be fatal to our mission."

"No," said Kirk. "In fact, I can probably go get them and be back for you by the time the inquest is over. I have a feeling the Rigelians are not very efficient about such things."

"Are you leaving now?" asked Spock.

"I hate to leave you and Teska down there all alone, but we don't have much choice."

"The needs of the many outweigh the needs of the few."

"I figured you would say that," answered Kirk. "Keep your communicator on you, and I'll see you in a few days. Kirk out."